For Better or Hearse

**Center Point
Large Print**

**This Large Print Book carries the
Seal of Approval of N.A.V.H.**

For Better or Hearse

LAURA DURHAM

CENTER POINT PUBLISHING
THORNDIKE, MAINE

This Center Point Large Print edition
is published in the year 2006 by arrangement with
Avon Books, a division of HarperCollins Publishers.

The text of this Large Print edition is unabridged. In other
aspects, this book may vary from the original edition. Printed in
Thailand. Set in 16-point Times New Roman type.

ISBN 1-58547-763-X

Library of Congress Cataloging-in-Publication Data

Durham, Laura.
   For better or hearse / Laura Durham.--Center Point large print ed.
   p. cm.
   ISBN 1-58547-763-X (lib. bdg. : alk. paper)
   1. Large type books. I. Title.

PS3604.U735F67 2006
813'.6--dc22

                                           2006001017

For my amazing husband,
who makes my heart skip a beat.

Acknowledgments

I am forever grateful to everyone who was so kind and encouraging to a new author, especially the hard-working independent and mystery booksellers around the country, and the wonderful mystery fans. Special thanks to my friends and family, who turned out in droves: the Brocks, Boones, Stahlmans, Bettye Sullivan, and all the wonderful friends in Jackson, Pickens, and Natchez, Mississippi; everyone at The O'Neal School, the Country Bookshop, and all the Southern Pines friends who made my homecoming so special; my wedding cohorts in DC, who keep me supplied with war stories: Jenny, Ric, Steve, Anne, Nick, Monte, Jim, Laura, Justine, Diana, Andrea, Lisa, Peter, Christine, and The Mafia Girls; Gillian, Wendy, and all my great girlfriends, who spread the word like wildfire; my writing buddies: Noreen (my invaluable mentor), Carla, Sandi, Donna, Val, Peggy, Ellen, Susan, Barb, The Mystery Chicks, and The Goffman Group. Thanks to my wonderful agent, Peter Rubie, the fabulous folks at Avon: Jeremy, Danielle, and my amazing editor Sarah Durand. Special appreciation to my parents, James, Liz and Lua (who were all publicity machines), my mother for joining me on my first book tour, my wonderfully supportive husband, and my brand new daughter and budding mystery chicklet, Emma.

Chapter 1

"I barely escaped being sliced up like a sushi roll, Richard." My shaking hand pressed the cell phone to my ear as I paced the marble lobby of the Fairmont Hotel. "I'm not exaggerating, either. Chef Henri tried to kill me."

The only thing worse than working with a temperamental bride is dealing with a temperamental chef, and as one of D.C.'s top wedding planners, I'd had my share of both.

"He refuses to serve the Peking Duck as a passed hors d'oeuvre, but with all these additional guests, we don't have room to do it as a station." I'd called my best friend, and arguably the city's best caterer, Richard Gerard, for some insight into the mind of a culinary despot. While I had a wedding at the Fairmont Hotel, Richard had one at the Dumbarton House in nearby Georgetown. His guests weren't due to arrive for another hour, and I could hear the clattering sounds of setup in the background.

Richard let out a high-pitched shriek. "We do not throw things, people. If I see anyone else tossing my imported Hungarian salad plates on the tables, heads will roll." He switched to his most calming voice. "Now Annabelle, you know he has a valid point. The real art of Peking Duck is in the carving."

I should never have asked for practical advice from someone who matched the food at a dinner party to the outfit he planned to wear.

"Richard, he chased me out of the kitchen with a knife and threatened to walk off the event if I ever set foot in there again."

"He's a chef. They're known for being dramatic, especially this one." A gasp. "Who put this cloth on the sweetheart table? I specifically requested the linen pin-tuck for the bride and groom, not the satin stripe."

I tapped my square-toed black pump in rapid fire. "I've about had it with chefs. I knew Henri had a reputation for being difficult, but I had no idea he would be so evil."

"You think you've seen evil?" Richard gave a low whistle. "You should hear the stories his former employees tell."

I didn't have time for Richard's stories now. They usually involved at least one person wearing something "totally wrong for them" and ended up with Richard giving an impassioned speech worthy of an Oscar.

"Okay, I get it, but what am I supposed to do?" I walked to the heavy glass doors leading from the lobby to the Colonnade room and glanced at my watch. The guests would be arriving from the church in a few minutes, and I had a chef who had threatened to walk off the job if I questioned his creative control again.

"Where's Kate? Maybe she could bat her eyelashes at him and he'd be a little more agreeable." Richard referred to my faithful assistant. Faithful to me, that is, not to any man she'd ever known.

"At the church. Anyway, I think it would take a bit more than eyelash batting to calm Chef Henri down."

I walked into the Colonnade and smiled. I often described it to my brides as "dramatic, yet feminine," and it ranked as one of my favorite ballrooms in the city. Walled entirely in glass, it looked out onto an open air courtyard that had a massive granite fountain and brightly colored flowers that were changed according to the season. At the moment, they were vibrant autumn shades of yellow and orange.

Inside, waiters lit votive candles around the ledge of the raised gazebo that took up the center of the room. Garlands of red roses curved around the gazebo's whitewashed columns, and tiny rosebuds strung on transparent thread hung between them to create a delicate curtain effect.

The bride had wanted to use elements from her Chinese background to personalize her wedding, so we'd incorporated lots of red, the Chinese color of celebration, and used signs from the Chinese zodiac in everything from the invitations to the ice sculptures. Huge mounds of deep crimson roses sat in the middle of each square table on crisscrossed red satin runners, and menu cards personalized with each guest's zodiac sign had been tucked into the napkins.

Two giant ice carvings, a tiger and a rabbit, rose up from huge blocks of ice and faced each other across the room. The ice tiger stood on its hind legs with his two front paws extended, and represented the groom's zodiac sign, while the rabbit had been carved in profile on its hind legs and represented the bride's sign. The sculptures were lit from above with beams of white light, and they glistened like fine crystal. Despite my usual distaste for ice sculptures, I had to admit that the room was striking.

"I swear these waiters are going to push me over the edge. I don't think a single one read the look book I put together for this event." Richard's voice crackled at me through static. "Are you still there, darling?"

"I'm admiring my handiwork, that's all." I walked back out into the hallway that led to the Colonnade.

"Is this the same little wedding planner who didn't think she could compete with the grand dames of the industry only a couple of years ago?" A gasp. "Flat-fold napkins, people, not fan-fold. This is not a Rotary lunch."

I adjusted the flower arrangement on the marble credenza next to the ladies' room and cradled the phone against my shoulder. Glancing in the mirror above the flowers, I brushed a long strand of auburn hair off my face. I pinched my cheeks to give them a bit of color and noticed that I actually had hollows now. The one advantage to having brides run you ragged—no time to eat!

"I've come a long way under your watchful eye, Richard."

"Don't mention it. Name your firstborn child after me and we'll call it even."

I laughed. "That's a safe promise since I haven't

even had a date in months." To be completely honest, I hadn't had a real boyfriend since I started Wedding Belles four years ago.

"Don't be down on yourself, darling. You've had some nibbles," Richard reassured me, and then his voice rose to a shriek. "What are the frosted champagne flutes doing *on* the tables? They're for passing only. Did anyone read their timeline?"

"By nibbles do you mean the pastry chef who had a lisp or the bartender who ended up taking home a bridesmaid?"

"Those are bad examples, Annie. What about the detective we dealt with on that murder case?" Glass shattered in the background. "If they broke my etched-glass water goblets, I'm going to die."

"Detective Reese?" I tried to play it cool, but I felt my face get warm at the thought of the dark-haired cop. We'd met when one of my former clients had turned up dead in the middle of the wedding reception and Richard and I had gotten tangled up in the investigation, much to the detective's dismay. I dismissed the fluttery feeling in my stomach when I remembered that I hadn't heard from the detective in the months following the case. Not that I'd expected to, of course. "When would I ever see him again? It's not like we run in the same circles."

Richard let out a breath. "Why wait for him to make the first move? Maybe you could happen to drop by the station and bump into him."

"That's not my style and you know it," I protested.

"I didn't know you had a style, darling."

I gave a fake laugh. "Very funny. What possible reason would I have to be at the police station? Unless I wanted to report one of my brides for harassment."

"Don't tell me bridezilla is still calling you at home all the time?"

"She called me last night at eleven o'clock to tell me that her honeymoon resort would be featured on a special segment of the news." I rolled my eyes. "I don't know how she got my home number in the first place."

Richard groaned. "I think that qualifies as grounds for a restraining order. When is her wedding, anyway?"

"I'll be rid of her in November, if I survive her neuroses that long. Only a couple more months." My call waiting beeped in, and I recognized Kate's number. "I've got to run. That's Kate on the other line calling from the ceremony." I clicked over and could hear lots of voices in the background.

"I just loaded the last trolley with guests and we're on our way. The first one should be there any minute. The videographer is on it, so maybe she can get room shots before most of the guests arrive."

"Good thinking, Kate." I hurried toward the hotel lobby so I could spot the old-fashioned open-aired trolley when it arrived. "I'll see you when you get here."

I dropped my phone into my jacket pocket and took out my crumpled wedding timeline. The photographer

14

had flown through the formal portraits, the limousines had been on time, and the bride had even been ready early. We were perfectly on schedule. I closed my eyes and let out a long breath. I knew not to trust the calm before the storm.

"Asleep on the job, are we?" A Scottish accent pulled me out of my momentary rest. My eyes flew open. His spiky blond hair and the tattoos that covered his arms were offset by a black muscle shirt and traditional red kilt. I wasn't an expert on formal Scottish attire, but I didn't think that leather, lace-up Captain America boots were usually part of the outfit.

The band. They had declined to go along with our theme, not that I could blame them. It wouldn't make much sense for an all-eighties rock band called "The Breakfast Club" to dress like geisha girls. The band agent had assured me that not everyone in the band wore kilts. The rest of the foursome sported leather pants, feathered hair, and Miami Vice jackets. Not your typical wedding band by a long shot.

He watched me give him the once-over and grinned. "We're dressed and finished with our sound checks."

I glanced at my watch. "That was fast." Usually bands took forever to set up.

Captain America gave me a wink. "We're good."

Uh-oh. Cute band guys were always trouble, especially if they knew they were cute. I could see it coming a mile away. By the end of the evening half of the bridesmaids would be all over this guy. I hope he didn't think I was falling for it. Before I could put on my I-mean-business wedding planner face, he reached out and touched my hair.

"Are you by any chance Scottish?"

"A bit," I found myself stammering. My usual composure had clearly abandoned me. "And some Irish."

He nodded and locked eyes with me. "I have a thing for redheads."

He turned and walked out of the lobby, looking back once to smile. My I-mean-business wedding planner face had been shot to hell, and I felt lucky just to keep my mouth from gaping open. The bridesmaids didn't stand a chance.

Usually Kate attracted most of the male attention at weddings with her bouncy, blond hair and come-hither heels. I'd been able to steer clear with sensible shoes and a general disregard for primping. I pulled my hair back into a quick bun as I gave myself a mental shake. I didn't have time to get flustered by a bad boy musician who probably flirted with everyone. Even if he did have a thing for redheads.

"They're right behind me." Fern dashed through the front doors waving a hairbrush. He wore his dark hair in a tight ponytail, and I suspected he'd coordinated his red brocade jacket to go with the decor.

Fern had become known as the wedding hair guru in Washington because of his attentiveness to brides. He insisted on doing the final touches only moments before the bridal processional, and he always waited until after the ceremony to repair his masterpieces. Sometimes I feared that he would actually start walking down the aisle with the bride, hair spraying in time to the music.

Now, the ceremony over, Fern had beat a hasty retreat from the church to the Fairmont. He ran past me, blowing me an air kiss with one hand. "I have to find my equipment case before the bride arrives. I barely beat the trolleys over here."

Sure enough, the orange and gold Old Town Trolley pulled up in front of the glass doors, and guests began emptying out. I met the videographer as she came through the doors, battery packs and wires barely peeking out from under her black suit jacket. One of the few female videographers in the city, Joni was also one of the most talented and the most chatty. I had to be careful or I'd find myself gabbing with her for half an hour.

"Hey, Joni. We're in a big rush. Could you get some shots of the courtyard before the guests wreck everything?" I pointed out the enormous arrangement of red tulips by the door to the outdoor courtyard and the masses of red rose blooms we'd floated in the fountain. "Then once you've got that, you can go inside to the Colonnade. The bride wants lots of detail shots of the ice sculptures."

"Wait until you see the footage I got of the bird loose in the church. I think the bride's aunt is still trying to get the bird poop out of her hair."

I cringed and made a mental note to look for the wet wipes in my emergency kit. I was sure they could handle bird poop.

"Can you show me later?" I gave her a prod toward the courtyard, where people were beginning to descend.

"Sure, just remind me." Joni also had the attention span of a fruit fly and she knew it. She hurried off past the guests, who were being distracted by the line of waiters offering trays of ginseng lemonade and green tea martinis, the specialty drinks for the evening. The pianist played tunes from *Madame Butterfly* in the background as guests mingled around the bar and moved outside to the courtyard. So far, so good.

Time to deal with Chef Henri. Taking a deep breath, I walked back into the Colonnade and went immediately into the kitchen, expecting to be greeted by the usual bustle of the waiters and grumbling of the chef. Nothing. All the waiters must have been passing hors d'oeuvres, and Chef Henri had probably decided to go off somewhere to pout. Perfect. A hundred eighty guests would be sitting down to dinner in less than an hour and I had no chef.

I stormed out the swinging exit door that led to the far side of the Colonnade and stopped short. Taking a few steps forward, I grabbed the back of a chair to keep my knees from buckling.

I had found Chef Henri.

I didn't know whether the blue tinge on his skin was connected to the blood that covered the lower part of his chef's jacket or was a result of his being impaled on the outstretched claw of the enormous ice tiger. All I knew was that he looked very cold and very dead.

Chapter 2

"A horrible crime has been committed!" Fern's shrieks carried across the room. Could he see across the room to where I stood in front of the dead, now dripping chef? "Where are you, Annabelle? My styling case has been stolen."

"I'm on the other side," I managed to call out. I could hear Fern's indignant footsteps, but I couldn't take my eyes off the impaled chef to turn around.

"Who do I speak to about lodging a complai . . . ?" Fern's voice trailed off as he walked up beside me. "Oh dear. Tell me this isn't the chef you had a fight with."

My mouth dropped open. "How did you know I had a fight with him?"

"Kate told me after you called her at the ceremony." He cocked his head to the side. "He doesn't look very good, Annabelle. Is he dead?"

I nodded my head and took a deep breath to keep from getting sick. I usually felt faint when I had to get my finger pricked at the doctor, and the sight of this much blood made my legs feel like cooked spaghetti.

"Poor fellow." Fern's expression was somber, then he nudged me with one elbow. "I must admit, honey, I didn't think you had it in you."

"I didn't do it!" I cried as I looked away from the body. "I found him like this."

Fern put a hand to his temple and slumped against

me. "Well, that's a relief. I was going to suggest some anger management courses, but if you're sure you didn't . . ."

I narrowed my eyes at him. "I'm sure."

"Of course I didn't really think you could do something like this. Even with all that stress you've got pent up from a severe lack of sex." Fern shook his head. I knew my lackluster love life scandalized him more than the dead body. "It would take a lot of strength to kill someone this way. What kind of ice sculpture is this?"

"A tiger. The groom's sign from the Chinese zodiac."

Fern walked close to the body. "So he's impaled on the tiger's arm?"

"The claws." I motioned to the sculpture without looking. "You can't see them anymore, but the tiger had big claws."

Fern raised an eyebrow. "That doesn't seem very safe."

"We didn't expect anyone to fall on them," I explained, trying to keep the irritation out of my voice.

"I hate to break it to you." Fern put his hands on his hips. "I don't think he fell. He had to have been pushed."

My head started to pound. "I need to sit down." I walked to the nearest table and pulled out a chair to collapse into. As unpleasant as Henri had been to me, I felt horrible that he had been murdered and a bit guilty for thinking such mean thoughts about him.

"Where is everyone?" Kate's voice carried from the doorway, and then I saw her blond head bobbing toward me. I nudged Fern to stand in front of the ice sculpture, so she wouldn't start screaming at the sight of the corpse.

Kate barely glanced up as she plopped down in the chair next to me and dropped her pink Kate Spade bag on the floor. She shrugged herself out of the jacket that covered the backless dress I'd forbidden her to wear. "Now don't get upset, Annabelle, but we might have to fly into the ointment."

"You mean a fly in the ointment?" Kate's ability to mangle even the most common expression scared me. Lately some of her word concoctions had started to make sense, which scared me even more. "We already have one."

"Why?" Kate's eyes widened. "Is Chef Henri still being impossible?"

Fern stepped away from the ice sculpture. "I wouldn't say that exactly."

Kate saw the body and jumped up, promptly losing balance on her stiletto heels and stumbling to the side. She gave a yelp as she fell, and I lunged to catch her. Fern moved neatly out of the way as the two of us went down, arms flailing. I lay on my back, assessing the possibility of serious injury, until I heard a familiar Scottish accent.

"Should I ask what you're doing down there or assume that you have everything under control?" I

21

looked up at the kilt-wearing band leader, who had one eyebrow raised and appeared to be stifling a great deal of laughter. Fabulous. He was a smart-ass, too.

"You could give me a hand if you have nothing better to do," I grumbled.

He winked at me as he pulled me up. "I can't think of anything that could be better."

Did women really fall for this? Kate, still on the ground, cleared her throat loudly and stared at the Scottish equivalent of David Bowie. Apparently they did.

Fern ignored Kate's protests as he pulled her up, and then turned to me. "What's with the kilt? I thought you said this wedding had an Asian theme."

"He's with the band," I explained, trying to keep the impatience out of my voice. Fern gave me a knowing look and nodded.

"What's with the kilt?" Kate practically screamed. "How about what's with the dead guy?"

"That's the chef." Fern put an arm around Kate. "The one Annabelle had the fight with, but she swears she didn't kill him. Between you and me, I don't think she has the strength to do it, anyway."

"I'm still in the room, you know." I rubbed my temples where my head had started to pound.

Kilt-boy inspected the corpse closely. "This isn't part of the decor?"

Fern gasped. "What kind of weddings do you have in Scotland?"

"American weddings are supposed to be really different and outrageous. Don't you have Renaissance themes and the like?"

"That's a very small, off-beat part of the population," I explained. "We certainly don't have murder-themed weddings. Not in Washington, at least."

"Can we continue this discussion somewhere away from Chef Henri?" Kate backed away, her voice trembling. "This is horrible. He's blue."

Fern shuddered. "I'm sure the ice is cold."

"I don't think frostbite is what got him." Kate rubbed her arms as if trying to warm herself. "I can't believe he's dead, even if he was impossible to work with."

I glanced at the pale lips and flat, expressionless eyes, then looked away and took a long breath. The man who had been such a terror to me earlier hardly seemed imposing now. Chef Henri had been far from beloved, but I wondered who hated him enough to do this.

"Annabelle, are you in here?"

"Richard?" I didn't know whether to be relieved or concerned. Richard usually didn't decrease the drama in a situation. "I'm on the other side of the gazebo."

"My event doesn't start for another hour, so I came over to try to help you out with Chef Henri. . . ." His words trailed off as he came into view of the spectacularly lit chef impaled on an ice tiger that was being inspected by a heavily tattooed Scotsman.

"Now, Richard," I said, then stopped. I didn't know where to begin. In this case, it was as bad as it looked.

"Oh my God." He put both hands to his head, without disturbing the dark, choppy hair that I knew he'd painstakingly arranged to look messy. "Can you explain this catastrophe?"

"Don't worry," Fern reassured him. "He's with the band."

Richard didn't take his eyes off the spectacle in front of him. "How long has he been here?"

Fern turned to me. "When did the band arrive?"

"I'm talking about the dead body hanging off that ice monstrosity." Richard kept his voice level, but his face had started to turn an unpleasant shade of pink under his spray-on tan.

"I found him like this a few minutes ago," I said. "I meant to call the police right away but Fern came in, then Kate got here, then the bandleader found all of us—"

Richard held up a hand to silence me. "So the police haven't been notified yet? Shall I help you move him onto the dance floor so guests could dance around him?"

Fern's eyes widened. "Oh, I don't think that's such a good idea."

So much for sarcasm. Richard cast his eyes heavenward and muttered under his breath.

"I'm telling you, Richard, we just found him," I insisted. "He can't have been dead very long."

Richard walked up to the chef as he pulled out his cell phone. "Are you people out of your minds? He's melting. I'm going to call the police before there's nothing left but a body balancing on an ice cube." He leaned in close to the corpse. "Is this Henri?"

"You mean the chef I had the big fight with that everyone seems to know about?" I glared at Kate, who began busily inspecting the carpet. "Yep. You can call me Miss Motive."

Richard closed his phone and the color drained from his face. "I didn't recognize him."

Fern gave a sad shake of his head. "He doesn't look his best, I'm sure. Which is a shame, because with the right haircut I'll bet he could look quite attractive."

"I know he wasn't the most popular chef in town but I didn't know anyone hated him enough to do this." Richard's voice caught in his throat. "This is not good, Annabelle."

"Thank you for noticing. At least no one from the wedding has seen him yet."

"Um, Annabelle." Kate tugged on my sleeve.

I turned around and found myself face-to-face with the bride. Crap. She let the cathedral-length veil that had been draped across her arm drop to the floor, and her dramatically made-up eyes were fixed on Chef Henri. I could be pretty sure this wasn't how she'd pictured her wedding day.

I opened my mouth to reassure her that everything would be fine, but I was too late. For such a petite, demure-looking girl, she could really scream. My hair stood on end as I clutched my hands over my ears, and I feared the glass walls of the room would shatter at any moment.

Richard jumped at the noise, and his phone flew straight up in the air. Reaching back to catch it, he stumbled into the corpse and the ice tiger teetered precariously on its base. As the massive sculpture began to lurch backward, Richard grabbed the chef to keep it from falling. The bride stopped screaming abruptly and her knees buckled as she sank to the floor. Fern caught her by the veil before she hit the ground.

"I think I might be sick." Richard put one hand over his mouth as the other clung to the dark, wet strands of hair that were once part of the dead chef's tragic comb-over.

"Hold on and I'll push from the other side." The bandleader took a few long strides around the ice sculpture.

"Stop right where you are," a deep voice boomed from behind us. I spun on my heels and saw a uniformed police officer with a hand above his holster. "Nobody move."

I looked on helplessly as the bride's veil gave way and she hit the carpet face first with a soft thud, leaving Fern holding a handful of white tulle. Richard let out a barely audible squeak before Chef Henri's hair slipped through his fingers and the giant ice tiger crashed to the ground, corpse and all.

Chapter 3

"I say we make a run for it," Kate said under her breath. "I'll create a distraction and you guys sneak out the back."

Kate, Fern, and I sat at a round cocktail table draped in an ivory hotel tablecloth while Richard paced in front of us. The walls of the basement meeting room had been upholstered in a silk cream damask to coordinate with the patterned carpet and match the linens. Hotels were big on neutrals.

We'd been stashed in the Imperial Room while we waited to be questioned, but it had been ages since they'd taken the bandleader to talk to a detective. The silver pitcher of water they'd set out had been empty for an hour, and my stomach had started to rumble.

"One problem with that plan," I replied. "We don't know how to get out the back. I've never been in through the loading dock, have you?"

"What a splendid idea, Kate." Richard's voice had a tone of mild hysteria to it. "I, for one, am all up for adding 'fugitive' to our résumés."

"I'm sure we aren't really suspects." Kate stretched her arms over her head, causing her dress to inch dangerously high up her thighs. Not that she cared. "This is just a formality because we found the body."

"Don't you mean found the body, touched the body, ruined the crime scene, and destroyed evidence?" Richard counted off on his fingers.

She rolled her eyes. "If you want to get really technical about it . . ."

"We're staying right here until this mess is sorted out," Richard said firmly. "Anyway, the four of us would get all of two blocks out of the city before being arrested."

"What do you mean?" Fern protested. "We can blend in."

Richard looked Fern up and down. "Are those Prada loafers?"

Fern nodded enthusiastically and held up his feet so we could all get a good look at his designer shoes. "Do you like them in red?"

Richard folded his arms across his chest. "I rest my case."

Kate slumped back down in her chair. "I guess that plan is up the window."

"*Out* the window," Richard and I said in unison.

The door opened and the uniformed officer we'd met previously strode into the room. A dark-haired man wearing beige pants and a navy blazer followed, closing the door behind him. Detective Reese. He looked exactly as I remembered him, though a little more tan.

"Well, well, well." He pulled a chair out and sat down facing us. "The gang's all here."

Richard looked even more jumpy since Reese had entered the room and he gave a nervous giggle. "You're on this case?" The last time we'd encountered the detective, Richard's business had been shut down and he'd almost been arrested.

"Lucky me, right?" Reese gave me a quick glance then opened his small leather notebook. So much for the sight of me causing him to swoon. I wondered if he even recognized me.

"Would you like me to tell you what happened, Detective?" I felt a hint of irritation creep into my voice. "It might save you some valuable crime-solving minutes."

He looked up and held my gaze with his deep hazel eyes. The corner of his mouth twitched up into a half smirk. "I'm glad to see you're as easygoing as ever, Miss Archer."

I felt a flush begin to move up my neck. "I didn't know you remembered me, I mean, us."

Reese looked from me to Kate to Fern and settled on Richard. "Vividly."

"I had nothing to do with it," Richard burst out. "When I came in the room, they were all standing around the body."

I shot him a look. "Thanks, Richard."

Reese nodded and flipped to a page in his notebook. "So how did you end up holding the deceased 'by the hair' and dropping him onto the floor?"

"I tried to catch him and ended up with a handful of hair." Richard paled a few shades.

"That comb-over was the real crime," Fern muttered.

Reese turned his attention to Fern, who shrunk back into his chair. "When did you enter the crime scene?"

"You see, I'd just realized that my equipment case was missing and went to find Annabelle so I could report it stolen." He took a quick breath and leaned forward. "When I came into the Colonnade, I saw her in front of the ice sculpture."

The detective wrote quickly in his pad. "Did you see anyone else in the room?"

"Well, the chef." Fern shrugged. "But he was dead, so I don't think he counts."

"No, he doesn't count." Reese sighed and turned to Kate.

"I must have come in after that because Fern and Annie were both in the room, but I didn't notice the body at first." Kate adjusted one of the spaghetti straps of her dress. "The band guy came in right after me. Probably not more than two minutes later."

Reese asked the uniformed officer to bring in the lead singer, and then looked at his notes. "So if I have this right, Annabelle came in, followed by Fern, Kate, the band guy, then Richard."

"Ian," the kilt-clad Scotsman said from the doorway. "Not that I mind 'band guy.'"

Reese gave Ian the once-over and turned to me. "This is the lead singer of the wedding band?"

I smiled and nodded. "They're supposed to be very good."

"We're better than good, darling." He came in and pulled up a chair next to me. "It's a shame you didn't get to check us out." Ian didn't seem to be intimidated by the police presence, or even notice it, actually.

30

I tried not to blush more than I had already.

Reese looked between us for a second, and then went back to his notes. "We're trying to piece together tonight's chain of events. When did you come into the room?"

"After I spoke to this lovely redhead in the lobby, I went to check on how the rest of the band was coming along." Ian turned his gaze from me to the detective. "Maybe ten minutes later I went into the reception room and saw the two girls on the floor and the chap in the great jacket standing next to them. The high-strung fellow didn't come in until after that."

Richard twitched visibly, and Fern puffed his chest out.

Reese raised an eyebrow at me. "What were you doing on the floor?"

"I got startled when I saw the body and stumbled over my shoes," Kate said before I could explain. She held her legs out to show the detective the high heels. Clearly, Kate needed more male attention. "Annabelle tried to catch me, but we both ended up on the ground."

Reese turned back to me. "It seems that you were the only person alone with the body, then."

"Aside from the person who killed him, you mean?" I didn't like the way this seemed to be headed.

"Of course," the detective said quickly. "Did you see anyone leaving the room?"

I shook my head. "But someone could have left through the kitchen and escaped through the back of

31

the house without anyone seeing them. Anyone who worked in the hotel knows how to get around in the back corridors."

Reese arched his eyebrows. "The back of the house?"

"Sorry." I gave an apologetic smile. "That's the term we use for all the behind-the-scenes areas like the kitchen and the corridors that connect everything."

"Have you ever been in back?"

"Sure," I admitted. "I've gone into the kitchens and the employee cafeteria before. But I wouldn't know how to get around easily, if that's what you're getting at."

"Were you in the back at all today?" Reese sounded casual, but red lights started going off in my head.

I sat up on the edge of my chair. "I went into the kitchen to check on things and discuss the setup with the chef."

Reese didn't look me in the eyes. "When did this take place?"

"About half an hour before I found him murdered." My mouth felt very dry. Did they think I killed Chef Henri? "But I stayed in the lobby from the time I left Henri in the kitchen to when I came back in the room. I'm sure lots of people saw me."

"I can vouch for her being in the lobby." Ian gave a firm nod of his head. He looked at Reese seriously and almost appeared fierce. "If you think this girl murdered someone, you're all wrong, mate."

I gave Ian a grateful smile, and then glared at Reese.

"See? What does my being in the kitchen have to do with Henri's death?"

"It seems that one of the other chefs overheard you having a huge fight with Henri earlier today and said that you left in a rage." Reese snapped his notebook shut and stood up.

I cringed. "We had a disagreement over one of the food stations. Who said I left in a rage?"

"The same person who called us to report the murder." Reese finally met my eyes. "And named you as the killer."

Chapter 4

"That's impossible!" Leatrice Butters, my elderly neighbor who took an overeager interest in my personal life, had been waiting for me at the door of our narrow Georgetown apartment building when I got home from hours of police questioning. She wore a navy sweatsuit with green puffy frogs that seemed to squeak each time she pressed against one. Leatrice had a fondness for "action" clothing. "Who could ever suspect you of murder?"

Richard had insisted on making sure I got home safely and had walked ahead of me up the stairs to open my door. I'm sure it had nothing to do with getting out of earshot of Leatrice and her squeaking frogs.

"Apparently some overeager cook saw me right

after I found the body and assumed I did it." I already felt weary explaining the night's events and dreaded having to do it a hundred more times. "Once the police pinned him down, he admitted that he didn't see me doing anything but standing next to the body."

"Thank goodness for that." Leatrice looked relieved as she followed me closely up the stairs to my fourth floor walk-up. The building was only four stories high, with two apartments on each floor. Small enough for neighbors to actually know each other, which was rare in D.C. Sometimes I considered it more of a mixed blessing, though.

"How did you know about the murder before we got here?" I turned to Leatrice as we reached my floor. "It hasn't been on the news, has it?" My brides would be less than thrilled to see me on the news involved in a murder. The fact that the murder took place at a wedding would send some of them into comas.

Leatrice shook her head and beamed. "My police scanner. I keep it on all the time."

I felt my stomach drop. So much for keeping this incident hushed up. "You heard my name on a police scanner?"

"No, dearie." Leatrice patted my arm. "I heard that the report came from the Fairmont and remembered that you mentioned the hotel when I saw you leave this morning. To be honest, the scanner doesn't give as much information as I'd hoped."

"Really?" Knowing Leatrice, she'd been expecting color commentary of the crimes. I needed to lie down.

Richard held the door open for me and visibly restrained himself from shutting it on Leatrice. According to Richard, Leatrice meddled in my life too much. I don't think he liked the competition.

I dropped my purse on the floor and collapsed onto my slightly worn yellow twill couch. Nudging a pile of wedding magazines out of the way, I propped both feet up on my coffee table. Leatrice sat down next to me while Richard headed off to the kitchen.

"So who do they think did it?" Leatrice's eyes danced with excitement. Sometimes it worried me how much she liked mysteries.

"I have no idea." I let out a deep sigh. "Considering how many people hated the murdered chef, it could have been anyone. Apparently I had the least motive of anyone in the hotel."

"I told you, Annabelle." Richard emerged from the kitchen with a miniwheel of brie and a box of crackers. "Anyone who ever worked with Henri wanted to kill him. He was the most notorious chef in town. And one of the most talented."

Leatrice put a hand on my arm. "Is that cute detective working the case?"

Richard snickered, and I glared at him. "Yes, Leatrice, but I've told you a thousand times that there's nothing going on there."

"I know." Leatrice's face fell. "It's such a shame."

"Isn't it, though?" Richard gave me a sugary smile as he sat down across from us in the matching yellow armchair. Richard loved seeing me squirm when

Leatrice started trying to play matchmaker. I'm sure it was the only reason he tolerated her. He put the box of crackers on the table and started to open the brie.

"I don't know if I would eat that cheese." I cringed as Richard opened the round wooden box. "I think I've had it for a while."

Richard unwrapped the white paper covering and made a face. "Now you do understand that the refrigeration process does not stop time, don't you?"

"Yes." I rolled my eyes. "I just forgot about it."

Richard stood up, holding the offending cheese in front of him at arm's length. "I will never understand how you can be so detailed and precise with your weddings, yet your own life is a mess."

"It is not a mess," I protested. "Anyway, if I spent all my time shopping and cleaning, I'd never be able to put in the hours to plan all those perfect weddings."

"One word for you, darling." Richard disappeared into the kitchen then poked his head up over the counter that separated the living room and kitchen. "Balance."

"I have balance," I shouted over my shoulder as I sunk into the couch. "I'm even taking a yoga class. If that isn't balance, I don't know what is."

Richard walked back into the living room and planted his hands on his hips. "You're taking yoga? Miss Type A, if-I'm-not-doing-ten-things-at-once-I'm-not-busy? Now this I have to see."

"Fine." I folded my arms across my chest.

"Now, now." Leatrice waved her arms. "You kids

stop your bickering. You're just like me and my Jimmy used to be."

Jimmy? Richard mouthed to me.

"Her late husband," I said under my breath.

Richard's eyebrows shot up and he opened his mouth to say something, but I grabbed him by the sleeve. I stood and began tugging him into the kitchen.

"Come on; let's go find something to eat." I turned to Leatrice. "We'll be right back."

Once we got into the kitchen, Richard pulled my hand away and started unwrinkling his sleeve. "What was that all about? Doesn't she know by now that the chances of us getting together are slim to nil? Heavy on the nil?"

"I think she forgets things sometimes. I'm not going to be the one who explains things to her again. You do it."

Richard wagged a finger at me. "I have a strict 'don't ask, don't tell' policy."

"People have to ask? I mean, aside from Leatrice?"

"Very funny, Annabelle." Richard narrowed his eyes and looked over the counter at Leatrice, who was happily pressing the frogs on her shirt to make them squeak. "I think the nut-ball has a selective memory."

"Be nice, Richard."

He pressed a hand over his heart and let his mouth gape open. "You wound me, darling. When am I not nice?"

"Well . . ." I began.

Richard cut me off with a raised palm. "That was a

hypothetical." He opened the refrigerator as the door-bell rang. We both jumped at the loud noise.

"Could you get that Leatrice?" I called out as I turned to examine our food options.

"Of course, dearie." She shuffled to the door. "Are you expecting anyone?"

Leatrice opened the door and gave a small scream. Richard and I both froze.

"Good heavens," Leatrice gasped. "We're being robbed!"

Chapter 5

I rushed into the living room and saw Leatrice with her hands in the air and Ian standing in the doorway with a puzzled expression on his face. I didn't see a weapon in sight.

"Leatrice, what are you talking about?" I went up and pulled her arms down. I heard Richard's muffled laughter behind me. "Ian isn't robbing us."

"You know him?" Leatrice flushed. "I guess I got startled by the tattoos."

"Sorry about that." I waved Ian into the room. He'd traded in his kilt and Captain America boots for a pair of broken-in jeans and Doc Martens, but he'd kept the black tank top. If it weren't for the tattoos covering both well-muscled biceps, he'd be practically main-stream.

"Are those real?" Leatrice had overcome her embarrassment and stood inches away from Ian's arms.

He nodded. "Do you like them?"

Leatrice cocked her head to one side. "They're interesting. This woman certainly isn't dressed to be riding a dragon like that, though."

"Tattoos are very fashionable now." Richard sank onto the couch, barely taking note of the body art. "Everyone has them."

"Do you think I should get one?" Leatrice brightened.

"No," I said forcefully. I noticed Richard's disappointment that I wouldn't let him egg her on and glared at him. I turned my attention to Ian. "What are you doing here, by the way?"

He produced my boxy, metal wedding emergency kit from behind his back and set it on the floor. "The lads accidentally loaded this in with our equipment. Your address is on the business card you taped to the inside, so I figured I'd return it to you."

"Thanks." I wondered if that was the only reason he'd returned it personally, but I didn't want to take a bit of harmless flirting too seriously. He seemed like the type who did lots of flirting anyway.

Ian took a few steps away from Leatrice and gave my apartment the once-over. "Is this just an office or do you live here?"

"I live here," I explained. "My office is down the hall with the bedroom." My apartment was shaped like a baby rattle with two clusters of rooms separated by a long hallway. I loved the fact that nothing in

Georgetown was a standard size or shape.

He strode over to the windows that lined the front of the living room and pulled back the curtains. He peered three stories down to the street. "Great location."

"It's a very safe building." Leatrice followed him across the room. "I'm president of the neighborhood watch." Actually, Leatrice *was* the neighborhood watch.

"How did you get in, anyway?" I asked. The front door was controlled by a keypad. You either had to know the code or have a resident buzz you in.

He gave me a lopsided grin and shrugged.

"On second thought, I don't want to know." I looked at my watch. "Did you just leave the hotel?"

"The police made our load-out a bit longer than usual. At least they didn't make us wait until they'd questioned everyone or I'd still be there."

Leatrice raised herself up on her tiptoes, which still only brought her chest level to Ian. "You were at the murder scene, too?"

"Bit of bad luck, eh?" He flashed her a smile. I could tell that Leatrice didn't think it was bad luck at all.

Leatrice moved in close. "Did you see anything important? Any clues?"

"Lots of people coming and going all day, but nothing sinister." He placed his hands on the back of an oversized armchair and leaned forward. "I don't see how they're going to sort this mess out with everyone looking the same."

"What do you mean?" Leatrice asked.

"Except for me and the lads, everyone at that place is dressed alike. All those waiters are in tuxedos and the cooks are in those white jackets. Who can tell them apart?"

"I never thought of it that way," I said. "But not everyone is a suspect, are they?"

"The police spent a lot of time with the kitchen staff," Ian said.

"That makes sense." Richard picked at a tiny blob of something on my couch. I needed to stop using my couch as a dining table. "They did work with Henri the most and had the easiest access to him."

"But who would benefit the most from his death?" Leatrice tapped her chin. "The killer has to have a strong motive."

"Trust me, Leatrice." I patted her on the arm. "Anyone who knew the victim had a strong motive."

"The only time I saw the chef that day, he was dead." Ian sidestepped around the chair he'd been leaning on and sat down. He propped his feet on my coffee table, then noticed Richard shooting daggers at him and dropped them back to the floor. "So I guess that leaves me out."

Leatrice folded her arms across her chest and her frogs let out a chorus of squeaks. "Not necessarily. You could have a secret motive."

"Oh, please," Richard mumbled, then pointed to the unidentifiable spot on my sofa and whispered to me, "What on earth have you been doing on here?"

41

"Nothing." I could feel my face warm. "I probably spilled something."

"A secret motive would make you the perfect killer." Leatrice raised her voice to talk over us.

"You do have a dining table, you know." Richard looked behind him at the wooden table covered in paperwork then let out a long breath. "Forget I said anything."

I glanced at Ian and he caught my eyes, then winked at me and grinned. Richard cleared his throat and I looked away.

Don't even think about it, darling, Richard mouthed to me. I didn't have to be an expert lip reader to understand his meaning.

"What if you had a connection to the victim that no one knew about?" Leatrice ignored us and continued. "If no one knows your motive, then you wouldn't even be a suspect."

"I suppose that's true." Ian shifted in his chair, clearly humoring Leatrice. "But the chef was dead when I saw him."

"Ah ha!" Leatrice pointed a finger at Ian. "You knew he was a chef, though."

Ian gave me a panicked look. "He wore a chef's hat and a jacket that said 'Chef Henri' on it."

"Oh." Leatrice sounded deflated.

Richard stood up and brushed trace amounts of lint off his pants. "I'm going to excuse myself before you get out the stretching racks and make this a proper inquisition. I've had quite enough questioning for one day, thank you."

"Do you really have to go?" I motioned to Leatrice and Ian with a jerk of my head as I followed him to the door and gave him a desperate look. Leatrice could continue like this for hours.

"It's nothing you can't handle, darling," he assured me, visibly stifling a laugh. "Anyway, I have to prepare for the bridal open house tomorrow afternoon."

I smacked my forehead. "That's tomorrow?"

"You and Kate told me you were coming a week ago, so don't even think of backing out." Richard wagged a finger at me.

"Why are you doing this again?" The thought of a roomful of prospective brides and their mothers sent a chill down my spine.

"Simple. The brides come to the showroom, they taste the food, ooh and aah over the stunning linens I've chosen, and then realize they absolutely must have me to cater their wedding."

I sighed. "It's in the afternoon, right? I have yoga in the morning."

Richard raised an eyebrow. "I already see problems with this new Zen quest of yours."

"We'll be there," I promised, making a mental note to call Kate as soon as he left. "It slipped my mind with all of this murder business. It's not every day I'm a suspect in a police investigation."

"Welcome to my world," Richard grumbled, picking up his briefcase from beside the door.

"Oh, please," I groaned. "You were a suspect for

about half a second and that was months ago."

Richard pressed his hand to his chest. "I may not seem wounded to you, but the scars run deep."

"This isn't the first time you've been involved with the police?" Ian called from across the room. He must have been desperate to get away from his conversation with Leatrice. "You've got more of a past than I imagined."

"Not really." I shook my head and felt my face flush. I could feel Richard's disapproving look. If I didn't know better, I'd have thought he was jealous. "One of our clients was murdered at a wedding a few months ago and Richard was a suspect for a few days."

Richard shot me a look. "For those of us who've been wrongly accused, a few days can feel like eternity. Now, as much as I'd love to stay and exchange criminal records, I've got to run." Richard gave Ian a slight nod, looked at Leatrice and sighed, then leveled a finger at me. "I'll see you tomorrow. And wear something nice. There'll be lots of brides attending."

"Of course." I started to close the door behind him.

Richard stuck his head back in. "Make sure Kate wears something modest. It's an all-ladies tea, so tell her not to waste the cleavage on us."

"Okay, okay." I pushed him out the door and sighed. Just what I wanted to do. Spend a Sunday afternoon chatting up brides. As if I didn't do enough of that already.

Chapter 6

"This isn't exactly how I imagined spending a Sunday off," Kate whined as I handed her one of two Grande Skim No Whip Mocha Frappuccinos and got in the passenger seat of her car. She'd double-parked in front of the Starbucks on Georgetown's bustling M Street, and taxicabs honked as they veered around her.

"I know." I'd barely closed the car door and balanced the drink between my knees when Kate careened the car out into traffic. "I'm missing my yoga class for Richard's bridal tea."

"Wasn't that class in the morning?" She glanced at the digital clock on her dashboard. "It's almost two o'clock."

I took a sip as Kate stopped for a red light. "I didn't want to cut it too close. Anyway, it took me forever to figure out an outfit." Actually, the thought of wrapping myself into a human pretzel had seemed far less appealing as I lay in bed this morning than it had when I'd signed up for Beginner Yoga. I'd only missed three classes, I reasoned with myself, ignoring the fact that there had only been four total.

"Annabelle, you're wearing a wrap dress. How hard is that?"

I tugged the beige fabric of the low wrap neckline together. "Well, I had to shave. And not only my ankles like when I wear pants."

Kate made a right turn without signaling and the

cars behind us screeched to slow down. "At least that explains why you don't have a boyfriend."

I glared at her as we bounced over the uneven pavement of the latest street construction, and I clutched my drink to keep it from spilling. "Have I fired you yet today?"

Kate stuck her tongue out at me. I noticed that she'd actually taken my advice and skipped the usual cleavage display. Her white cowl neck top was practically prim, although her hot pink skirt had a side slit that revealed most of her thigh. I knew I should be grateful for any nod to modesty, so I ignored the skirt.

We passed a row of tiny restaurants and shops as we headed toward the Potomac. People lingered over brunch on one of the restaurant balconies, and my stomach growled at the thought of Eggs Benedict. I could be sure that the bridal tea would feature pretty, dainty food not even remotely as satisfying.

As we turned up K Street and skirted past Washington harbor under the bridge, I rolled down my window so I could enjoy one of the few days of perfect autumn weather in Washington. We exited off K Street and Kate merged into traffic without looking or slowing down. The wheels screeched against the pavement, and I knew we'd left tire marks and possibly an accident behind us. I sunk a little lower in my seat and clung to the seat belt with my one free hand.

We passed the Watergate Hotel, all retro curves with fabulous views and even more fabulous scandal. On the other side, trees with burnished gold leaves edged the shores of the Potomac and colorful sailboats dotted the water. This was exactly the type of day that brought tourists in droves and made it impossible to get around. I looked at the rows of tour buses as we approached Memorial Bridge and shook my head.

"Richard will kill us if we're late."

"Relax." Kate pushed her sunglasses back on her head. "It's an afternoon tea. It's supposed to be fun."

"You call a roomful of brides and their mothers fun?"

"Good point."

"First a murder and now a bridal tea. I don't know which is worse."

"I'm surprised Richard didn't cancel the tea." Kate burned a red light to make a turn.

"Are you kidding?" I laughed. "The police know he had nothing to do with the murder. And you know Richard. Even if he were a suspect, he'd manage to pull off the event covertly."

"Right. What was I thinking?" Kate flipped her hair out of her face. "The police don't still think you had anything to do with the murder, do they?"

"No. Ian said they seemed to be most interested in the kitchen staff at the hotel."

Kate slammed on the brakes as the car in front of her stopped to take a photo of the Washington Monument out the window. "Ian?"

I pulled myself back from the dashboard. I didn't know whether my heart pounded from the near-death drive or the impending third degree. "You remember.

The lead singer from the band."

"The cute one with the tattoos? The one who is *so* not your type?"

"Why is he not my type?" I turned in my seat to face Kate. "I've dated wild guys before."

Kate raised an eyebrow and accelerated the car. "Who?"

"Steven in college. He was an environmental protester always chaining himself to something."

"Please, Annabelle. I'll bet he wore a ponytail and wrote poetry, too." Kate rolled her eyes at me. "Sensitive ponytail boys are not wild. Moody, maybe. But not wild. Trust me." When it came to men, I usually did.

"I never said I was interested in Ian, anyway."

"But you've talked to him since the wedding?" Kate screeched to a stop to let a tour group wearing identical bright orange T-shirts cross the street next to the Smithsonian Castle. She gunned the engine as the last person crossed.

"He came by my apartment yesterday." I held up a hand when I saw the "I told you so" look on Kate's face. "Just to return my emergency kit. It got mixed up in the band's equipment."

"Okay, so you're completely uninterested in this hot musician who came by personally to return your stuff. Got it. Please continue."

I ignored her sarcasm. "As I was saying, Ian thought the police spent a lot of time with the cooks."

Kate weaved her way through traffic to make all the

green lights, passing the row of massive Smithsonian museums leading up to the Capitol. "Which makes sense. They would have had more motive and opportunity than anyone."

"But there are so many of them, and they all dress alike." I took a final sip of my frappuccino and put the empty plastic cup in the armrest holder. "How will we tell the suspects apart?"

Kate gave me a sideways glance. "Why would we have to tell them apart?"

"We won't," I said quickly. "I'm a little curious about who hated Henri enough to impale him on an ice sculpture, that's all."

"If the police just cleared me as a suspect, I wouldn't want to cause any more trouble." Kate began scanning the streets for parking as we drove through the Capitol Hill business district. "But that's me."

"I have no intention of stirring up trouble." I pointed to a marginally legal parking space on Eleventh Street right across from Richard's town-house showroom. "I only said I'm curious. Georgia and Darcy will be able to tell us more."

"You mean Georgia and Darcy from the Fairmont?"

I nodded and looked out the window, pretending to be inspecting the parking space intently. "We're having lunch with them tomorrow."

"Well, well, well." Kate drummed her fingers on the steering wheel. "You didn't waste much time sticking your hose in this murder case."

"It's not my *hose,* it's my *nose.* And I'm not sticking

it anywhere. We have lunch with Georgia and Darcy all the time. Georgia is one of my few friends from UVA who ended up in D.C., and the only one aside from me who isn't a lawyer or doctor."

"Didn't you meet in 'Wedding Receptions for Fun and Profit'?"

"Very funny. You know there's no such class." I shook my head. Kate loved to joke that UVA had a mythical wedding planning degree. I'm sure the university founders would be spinning in their graves if they could hear. Georgia and I liked to joke that we were living proof that you could make a good living with an English degree as long as your job had very little to do with your major.

"And so what if I'm a little curious about the investigation?" I asked.

Kate angled the car into the parking space and turned off the engine. "As long as you're just curious. Promise me you won't get us any more involved in this mess than we already are, okay?"

"Why would you think that I'd get more involved—"

"Annabelle," Kate cut me off and leveled a look at me.

I sighed. "Fine. I promise."

"Thank you." Kate let out a long breath. "I feel much better."

"Ready for a roomful of brides?"

"And their mothers?" Kate examined her lipstick in her visor mirror, and then flipped it up. "Bring it on."

Chapter 7

"Where have you been?" Richard met us at the tall double doors of the gray row house. The metal plate next to the door read RICHARD GERARD CATERING and had been added since my last visit. Not surprising. Richard loved making changes to the office decor so he could stay on the cutting edge. I had recently talked him out of repainting the entire building in a greenish brown hue called "Baby's First Summer," and he was still in a snit that I'd referred to his new favorite color as "Baby's First Diaper."

I glanced at my watch. "The party only started half an hour ago. What could possibly have gone wrong yet?"

"Wrong?" Richard gave a falsetto laugh and looked behind him. "Who said anything is wrong?"

Kate lowered her voice. "Are you feeling okay?"

"You've got to help me," he said through a fixed smile. "My best captain, Jim, couldn't come at the last minute because his flying squirrel got sick, so it's just me and the kitchen staff."

"A flying squirrel?" I exchanged a look with Kate. "Is it legal to have those as pets?"

Richard held up his hand and shook his head. "Don't ask. My life is a Fellini film today. Not to mention, these people are out of control."

"The brides or the mothers?" I peeked around Richard to assess the roomful of guests. About a

51

dozen or so women and one stocky man clustered around a table draped in a chartreuse silk cloth and decorated with china teapots full of pink peonies. Trays of open-faced tea sandwiches and miniature pastries surrounded the flowers and were the focus of the oohs and aahs coming from the guests. It was hard to see any reason for Richard's anxiety. Then again, Richard didn't need a reason.

He arched a brow. "Take your pick."

I took another look at the guests. "I hate to burst your bubble, but this is a dream event."

"Oh, really?" Richard jerked his head in the direction of the one man in the group, clearly a Father of the Bride who was built like a fire hydrant and wore a dark, double-breasted suit. "Do you have any idea who that is?"

Kate shook her head. "He doesn't have the look of a politician." Kate kept up with politics by dating plenty of political staffers. She may not have known anything about the issues, but she knew which states had the cutest interns.

"I wish he were a politician," Richard said with a sigh, then lowered his voice and gave me a meaningful look. "He's in trucking."

My eyes widened. "Do you mean . . . ?"

"The family business."

"And?" Kate looked between the two of us. "I don't see the problem with a family-owned trucking company."

"Organized crime, Kate," I hissed.

"Oh." Kate shrugged. "Leave it to D.C. to have an organization for everything."

"It's not an association," I started to explain, and then thought better of it. "Never mind."

"Mr. Constantino's daughter, Sophia, is getting married next year, and he wants it to be the wedding of the century." Richard dabbed at his brow. "I don't know if I can handle the pressure."

"You're the best, Richard." I gave his arm a squeeze. "Don't worry about it. What's the worst that could happen?"

"I could end up lying facedown in fresh cement, that's what."

"Doubtful. He's in trucking, not construction." I grinned.

Kate nudged him and smiled. "You could end up in a shipment of bananas headed for Canada, though."

Richard glared at Kate. "Now I feel much better."

"That's what we're here for." Kate fluttered her eyelashes.

"And for the free food." I eyed the tray of scones a waiter set out on the buffet. Richard's cream scones were heavenly and usually vanished in a matter of seconds. "I don't have a thing to eat at home."

"Shocking," Richard drawled as he motioned us into the main room. "I'm going to check on the kitchen." He spun on his heel and disappeared down the hall.

"Do you think we can get in, eat, and get out without actually having to talk to any brides?" Kate asked.

"Annabelle Archer?" My name was practically

screeched over the conversation, which came to a complete halt. A mother and daughter in matching pink and green plaid headbands and grosgrain belts ran across the room. Debbie and Darla Douglas. One of my upcoming June brides and her mother.

Debbie's wedding to Turner Grant III promised to be an event fit for the son of a Mississippi congressman and the daughter of a country club Lady Who Lunches. Darla had happily turned over all the wedding planning to me once she'd negotiated free-flowing mint juleps and a bourbon-tasting bar for the reception. Darla was my favorite mother of the bride because she was usually too soused to care what went on.

"Debbie and I were hoping we'd see you here." Darla leaned in for an air kiss, and I tried to avoid getting splashed by her cocktail. Leave it to Darla to procure a martini at an afternoon tea. I wondered if she'd actually brought her own.

"Mother and I were discussing your idea of using magnolia leaves everywhere for the wedding." Debbie gestured with her matching martini. "We think it's an adorable idea."

Darla rested a hand on my arm. "Do you think we could find a magnolia china pattern or would that be too much?"

The wedding had already passed "too much" months ago.

"Maybe we could use that new leaf plate at Perfect Settings for the salad course," Kate said. "It's shaped kind of like a magnolia leaf."

Darla glanced at Kate next to me and a look of surprise crossed her face. "Kate, dear. I didn't see you there."

How many martinis had this woman already gone through? Kate elbowed me, and I pressed my lips together to keep from laughing.

Debbie put a hand to her cheek. "I didn't recognize you in that turtleneck." I'm sure they'd never seen fabric even remotely close to Kate's neck before.

"You look practically Republican." Darla giggled.

Kate flinched. "It's technically a cowl neck—"

I cut her off in mid-sentence. "Have you tried the scones yet? They're one of Richard Gerard's signature items."

"We haven't gotten to the food." Darla's eyes flitted to the buffet, and then dismissed the bowls of cream and berries with a shudder. Darla would as soon let a scone pass her lips than she would drink her morning orange juice straight.

Debbie raised her glass. "We're on a liquid diet until the wedding."

"But you both look fabulous." I couldn't imagine either woman getting more willowy, and I'd bet the only nutrition Darla had gotten for years came from the garnishes in her drinks.

"I have to fit into my Monique Luillier slip dress." Debbie downed her drink in one final gulp.

I had visions of Debbie walking down the aisle in a narrow slip dress holding a bouquet, her father's arm, and a martini. Kate and I would need a drink after this wedding. Or during it.

"Can we get you anything from the bar?" Darla cooed as she peered at the lonely olive in the bottom of her glass. "Our drinks need a little freshening up."

"I think I'm going to start with some food, but thank you."

"Suit yourself, sugar." Darla patted my hand, and then teetered off across the room to the bar with Debbie close on her Ferragamo heels.

"I hope Richard didn't invite anymore of our clients to this," Kate whimpered. "We can't count on all of them to be drunk on a Sunday afternoon. I would hate to have to pull off a coherent conversation."

"I'm going to be incoherent if I don't eat soon," I whispered to Kate as I tried to see through the crowd to the buffet. "Are there any scones left?"

"I can't see." Kate grabbed my elbow and pulled me forward. "Follow me, and don't make eye contact with anyone."

We maneuvered past clusters of chattering brides comparing bridesmaid dress colors and swapping favor ideas. I crossed my fingers no one would recognize us. We reached the food display, and I breathed a sigh of relief when I saw several scones left on the tray. Maybe everyone at the party was dieting to fit into their wedding dresses.

Kate held up a heart-shaped scone. "Is this a theme or has Richard gone soft on us?"

I looked at the trays of heart-shaped cookies and tea sandwiches that filled the table from end to end. I placed a tiny butter heart on my plate and reached for a scone. "It's official. He's finally lost his mind."

Kate laughed and handed me a napkin.

"Can you believe this, Mother?" The girl next to me motioned at the food. I guess she wasn't a big fan of hearts, either.

"What is it now, Viola?" The woman beside her sounded less than patient.

"There isn't a thing here that's vegan."

"You're not still on that kick, are you? Don't think for a second that your father and I are paying for a wedding where you serve nothing but vegetables."

"How can you expect me to use my own wedding to exploit animals?"

Kate raised an eyebrow and edged away from them. I turned to get some whipped cream and saw that the bride had straight dark hair parted down the middle that almost reached her patchwork skirt. She wore no visible makeup and was in serious need of eyebrow maintenance.

Her mother, on the other hand, could've given Tammy Faye Bakker a run for her money. She stood about a head taller than her daughter and wore her shoulder-length dark hair in a bob that was sprayed to within an inch of its life. Her eyelashes had so many coats of mascara it was a wonder she could still blink, and her eyelids were layered in about a dozen shades of blue.

"Viola, you cannot have a vegan wedding. How will you have a wedding cake if you can't use dairy products or eggs?"

"I'm sure they can make wedding cakes with soy."

The mother sucked in air. "If you won't listen to me, then at least listen to an expert. The caterer said that one of the best wedding planners in the city would be here. She can settle it."

I froze in mid-dollop and dropped the spoon back in the whipped cream. This was exactly the kind of wedding that would make me want to throw myself off Memorial Bridge within a week. I turned to Kate and motioned her toward the kitchen. I had to find Richard so I could kill him for giving my name to the Odd Couple.

"But I didn't get any berries to go with my scone," Kate argued as I pushed her down the hall and through the swinging door of the kitchen. A massive chef with salt and pepper hair stood behind a metal table singing an operatic version of the *Green Acres* theme song as he stamped out tea sandwiches with a heart-shaped cookie cutter. Several other cooks scurried around him in matching white chef jackets.

"You can eat as much as you want as soon as you help me murder Richard."

"It's always work, work, work with you." Kate put a hand on her hip. "Fine, then. Let's get this over with."

I realized that the kitchen chatter had died, and I looked behind Kate at the row of cooks staring at us in silence. The head chef's thick black eyebrows had become a solid line across his forehead as he scowled at us. He looked much more menacing when he wasn't singing old TV theme songs, despite the red plastic cookie cutter in his hand.

"Oops," Kate gulped. "Out of the frying pan and into a friar."

Chapter 8

"I think there's been a misunderstanding." I backed away from the glaring row of chefs. "We were joking about killing Richard."

"We could never catch him, anyway." Kate laughed nervously. "He's way too quick for us."

I shot her a look. "Thanks. That helped."

The head chef studied us for a moment, and then broke into a smile. "I know you. You're the wedding planner friends." His voice was a deep rumble that filled the room.

I breathed a sigh of relief.

The chef returned to stamping out heart-shaped sandwiches. "He talks about killing you, too. It must be an inside joke." The other cooks smiled along with their boss before returning to work, and the kitchen filled with the sounds of chopping and clattering dishes.

Kate and I exchanged a look. That didn't sound comforting.

"What else does Richard say about us?" I let out a long breath. "And how did you know who we were?"

"I've seen you at a few weddings when you run back

in the kitchen for something, but we haven't met officially." He wiped his large callused hands on a dish towel and extended one for me to shake. "Chef Marcello."

"Right. Sorry." I shook his hand but felt like smacking myself on the head. Marcello. The renowned Italian chef Richard told me stories about. His moods were as legendary as his cuisine. "I get so focused when I'm working at a wedding that I don't remember anyone."

"Isn't that how we all are? My cooks can tell you how I get on a job." Marcello gave a deep belly laugh and looked at his staff. A smattering of nervous laughter followed, and he began humming the theme from *The Addams Family*. Marcello seemed friendly enough, but it didn't bode well that Richard considered him moody.

Kate leaned over the counter and gave the entire line of chefs a flirtatious smile. "He can't be as bad as the last chef we worked with."

Marcello stopped humming and arched an eyebrow. "I know every chef in this town. Let me guess." He grinned and continued cutting. "Someone in off-premise catering? The head chef at Ridgewell's?"

"Nope." Kate rocked back on her heels and shook her head. "A hotel chef."

"Maybe we shouldn't be talking about this," I muttered so only Kate could hear. She ignored me.

"A big hotel?" Marcello held the red plastic heart in midair.

"Pretty big. Not one of the huge convention hotels, though."

I cleared my throat. "I really don't think this is a good idea."

"I'll give you a hint. It starts with an F."

"Henri," Marcello hissed, and slammed the heart down onto the counter. The room went silent.

Kate raised a finger in the air. "Technically that's an H."

"He means Chef Henri," I whispered to Kate. "And from his reaction, I'd say he knew him."

"We all knew Henri." Marcello's voice rose several notches. "Everyone in this kitchen suffered under him at one time."

I looked around the room at the grim faces. "You all worked with Henri?" Nods and scowls.

"Almost every decent chef in Washington passed through Henri's kitchen at some point," Marcello explained, his face reddening. "And every one was grateful when they left. Henri was nothing but a tyrant."

"If everyone hated him, how did he stay in business?" I asked. "Wouldn't it be impossible to keep a staff?"

Marcello gave a rough laugh as low murmurs passed through the room. "He was ruthless. He would ruin anyone who crossed him or tried to leave."

"My experience with Henri is starting to look almost pleasant," I said to Kate.

"How did you know Henri?" Marcello's face was

starting to return to a normal color.

"We found his body." Kate gave a small shiver.

Marcello paused and appeared to compose himself. "You were at the wedding where Henri was killed?"

"It was our client's wedding," I said. "And ice sculpture."

"Our thanks to your client, then." Marcello smiled out of one side of his mouth, and his eyes flitted back to his work. So much for an outpouring of sympathy.

Richard burst through the door holding a flowery pink plate and skidded to a stop. He gaped at us. "What are you doing in here? I have a roomful of brides dying to talk to one of the top wedding planners."

"Yes." I folded my arms across my chest. "About that, Richard—"

"No time to discuss." Richard held up the plate of pale yellow cake to the chef. "Mr. Constantino insists that this isn't real Italian cream cake."

Kate jabbed a finger at him. "You tricked us. You didn't tell us you were planning on inviting our clients plus a roomful of the city's most dysfunctional brides."

"I don't know what you're talking about." Richard twitched his shoulders and avoided our eyes.

Marcello drew himself up to full height. "This Mr. Constantino thinks he knows Italian cooking better than I do?"

"Of course not," Richard said. "Let me explain."

"The granola and Tammy Faye?" I said, drumming

my fingers. "Explain that."

Marcello slammed his palm on the prep table. "I do not cook with granola. You tell Mr. Constantino that if he wants granola in an Italian cream cake, then he needs to find another chef."

"Oh God," Richard whimpered, putting his hand over his eyes. "I'm going to end up like Jimmy Hoffa. I can see it already."

"Is Jimmy Hoffa in catering, too?" Kate whispered to me.

"This is too much." Marcello threw his hands in the air. "First the talk of Henri, now someone is telling me how to cook. And with granola. My creative energy has been stifled."

"No." Richard dropped his hand from his eyes and his eyes grew wide with panic. "Not that."

"I'll be out back meditating." Marcello turned and marched out the back door. The remaining cooks exchanged helpless looks.

Kate shook her head. "Is there anyone who isn't New Age anymore?"

"What did he mean 'the talk of Henri'?" Richard faced me.

"Nothing really." I shrugged. "Kate may have mentioned that we were at the wedding where Henri died. Apparently Marcello knew him very well."

Richard gasped. "You brought up Henri in front of Marcello?"

"Why is that a problem?" Kate asked.

Richard began rubbing his temples. "Over ten years

ago Henri and Marcello were best friends and worked as sous chefs together at the Willard Hotel. Until they had a falling out."

My mouth fell open. "Why didn't you tell us before?"

"It wasn't relevant." Richard narrowed his eyes at me. "I never thought you'd come marching into my kitchen and start chatting about the latest murder."

"But that was over a decade ago," I said. "Chef Marcello can't still be upset. What was the falling out?"

"When the job as head chef opened up, Henri framed Marcello for stealing and got him fired."

Kate swallowed hard. "I guess Marcello holds a grudge."

"He is Italian," I said. "Grudges get passed down for generations." I wondered if the grudge had turned into more than that and Marcello had finally gotten his revenge.

"I resent that," Richard said. "I'm part Italian."

"Refresh my memory, Richard." I put my hands on my hips. "What did you do when one of the other wedding planners made an unflattering comment about your food?"

Richard opened and closed his mouth a few times, then mumbled out of the side of his mouth, "I paid a voodoo priestess in New Orleans to put a hex on her."

"I rest my case."

Kate turned to Richard, her mouth gaping open. "Did it work?"

He suppressed a smile. "She looks awful. Her hair

has gotten so thin it looks like cotton candy."

"Remind me not to make you angry." Kate put a hand to her own fluffy blond bob. "I didn't know there were hair thinning hexes."

Richard began to turn red. "It wasn't supposed to be a hair thinning curse, but apparently I wasn't specific enough."

Kate turned to me, looking thoroughly confused. "You think Marcello put a hex on Henri?"

"No." I lowered my voice so the other cooks couldn't hear me. "I don't think he hexed him. I think he may have murdered him."

Chapter 9

"Everyone is talking about the murder." Georgia Rhodes downed her champagne cocktail in one long gulp. The blond Fairmont catering executive had shoulder-length flipped-up hair that any Texas debutante would envy and curves that would make Marilyn Monroe jealous. Like Marilyn, she drank only champagne. Today she'd already had two glasses, and we'd just given our lunch orders.

"Any idea who did it?" I'd grown accustomed to asking Georgia for advice and insider information since I'd moved to Washington. Being a few years older than me, she'd taken me under her wing when I decided to start a wedding planning business. After my brief stint planning events for a high-powered

D.C. law firm, I thought weddings would be a breeze in comparison. Little did I know that brides make lawyers look like Mother Teresa.

I sipped my iced tea and waved a bee away from my leg. Because of the almost summery September weather, we'd opted for a table in the Fairmont's courtyard under a green market umbrella that shaded us from the midday sun, but not from the local insect population. Kate dodged as a bee flew across the table to where she and Georgia's assistant, Darcy O'Connell, sat.

I glanced past Kate at the garden courtyard, which had looked completely different only two days ago. The red paper lanterns that we'd suspended from the trees on Saturday were gone, and a single red rose bobbing in the fountain was the only reminder of the wedding. You'd never have guessed there had been a murder only steps away from where we sat.

"Has anyone been arrested?" Kate asked.

"No." Georgia dangled her high-heeled mule off her foot and smiled. "The talk's been about who's going to plan the celebration."

"Georgia, you're awful." Darcy shook her head at her boss and gave her a disapproving look over her wire-rimmed glasses. Darcy was one of those girls who never showed an inch of skin or wore a speck of makeup but managed to attract looks anyway. Kate called it the naughty librarian look, and she couldn't believe that anyone could be as prim and unassuming as Darcy appeared. She thought it must be a ploy to

66

attract men through reverse psychology. She hadn't appreciated when I suggested she try reverse psychology sometime.

Georgia and Darcy were the perfect example of opposites who worked well together. Georgia reeled in clients with her Southern charm, and Darcy attended to all the behind-the-scenes details so the events came off without a hitch. Since Darcy didn't like too much attention and Georgia loved to hog the spotlight, it worked perfectly.

"I'm only telling the truth." Georgia signaled to the waiter for another drink. "No one in this place liked Henri, including us."

"I feel bad saying things about Henri now that he's dead." Darcy twisted a piece of her long dark hair into a spiral with her finger. Her hair was stick straight except for the wispy bits in front that she constantly twirled. I wondered how she fought the urge not to put her hair up. I couldn't go ten minutes without pulling mine into a ponytail.

"At least you're not being hypocritical." Kate shrugged off her suit jacket and revealed a nearly translucent white blouse. She slipped the jacket on the back of her chair. I gave a cursory glance around the courtyard and breathed a sigh of relief that no men were sitting near our table.

"I'll admit that I hated him." Georgia crossed her legs and jiggled her foot in circles. "He never let me change a thing on his menus and he insulted all of my 'pinch-me cute ideas.' Would it have been so hard to match the food to the linens just once?"

"Sounds like he didn't make many friends around here," I said.

"That would be putting it mildly." Georgia cast a glance over her shoulder, and then continued in a hushed voice, "I think Henri's death was the best thing that could have happened to this hotel. Even the housekeepers were afraid to go to the employee cafeteria because they had to pass the kitchens. He tormented everyone."

"Do you think the police suspect anyone in the hotel?" I asked, matching her whisper.

Darcy and Georgia exchanged a brief glance, and then Georgia stared at her empty champagne flute. "We were all questioned, of course. But they questioned me a second time. I don't have a convincing alibi."

"Weren't you here in the hotel?" Kate asked. She sat up as a pair of waiters brought four oversized salads in wide-lipped bowls to the table. One of them almost dropped a bowl in Kate's lap when he got a glimpse of her blouse.

"That's right," I remembered. "I didn't see you much when we set up for the wedding."

Georgia pinched her eyes together, and her forehead creased into deep furrows. She picked up a white ramekin of dressing and drizzled a thin stream onto her salad. "I was in my office with the door closed. I needed to catch up with paperwork."

The table fell silent as we began eating. Georgia

hated paperwork and loved being in the middle of an event. I didn't buy it.

"You never do paperwork." Kate shifted to the side and winked at Georgia as a waiter attentively refilled her nearly full water glass. "Are you sure you didn't kill him accidentally?"

I rolled my eyes. "How do you accidentally impale someone on an ice sculpture, Kate?"

"I'm telling you, I was in my office doing paperwork," Georgia insisted, a flush creeping up her neck. "I didn't have a choice."

Darcy cleared her throat. "Our general manager gave Georgia a deadline for all of her financial reports. She had to turn them in by the end of the weekend or she'd get a bad review. I would have helped her but I don't know how to do all the reports yet."

"Mr. Elliott has it in for me." Georgia's eyes flashed with anger. "He's wanted to fire me ever since I took this job. He'll use any excuse to write me up."

"Write you up?" Kate stopped eating and held her fork in midair.

"They can't fire you without cause," Darcy explained. "They have to keep track of your mistakes, then when they get enough they can fire you."

"Yikes." Kate cringed.

I looked at Georgia over the top of my iced tea. "Why does Mr. Elliott want to fire you?"

"I refused to go out with him when I first started here."

69

"I thought dating someone in the hotel is forbidden," Kate said. Leave it to Kate to know the ins and outs of dating protocol in any D.C. locale.

"Who cares about that?" Georgia burst out. "Have you seen him? He has more hair in his ears than on his head. At least before he got the plugs."

I cringed. Not a pretty picture. "So you were a little behind in your work and he put the screws to you?"

Kate leaned over toward me. "She said she *wasn't* dating him."

I decided not to even attempt to explain and turned back to Georgia. "How far behind were you?"

"I hadn't even started. I told Darcy to make sure no one bothered me, and she promised to check on the wedding. I explained all this to the police, but they didn't seem too convinced. Darcy was the only person who can vouch for me, and even she didn't see me for a couple of hours."

"I wish I could give you an alibi." Darcy nibbled the edge of her lip. "If I'd come back up to check on you, the police wouldn't have any reason to consider you a suspect."

"Don't be silly." Georgia smiled weakly. "If only I'd dated our general manager, I wouldn't be in this mess."

"Just because you don't have an alibi doesn't mean you're an automatic murder suspect." I waved a forkful of greens. "The police have to have motive and evidence. If you weren't anywhere near the murder, there's no way they could link you to the crime."

"And if you were in your office then you were nowhere near the murder scene," Kate said. "Annabelle, on the other hand, spent half the day with the dead body and they don't consider her a suspect, even though she had more opportunity to kill Henri than anyone. And a pretty good motive, too."

"Remind me not to call you as a character witness," I said out of the corner of my mouth.

"What's your motive?" Darcy readjusted her glasses. "You barely even knew Henri."

"Not that you had to know him very long to despise him." Georgia took the flute of champagne out of the waiter's hand before he could place it on the table. "The argument we had about Peking Duck, although it was less of a disagreement and more of him chasing me out of his kitchen."

Georgia took a gulp of champagne. "Welcome to my world. He chased me out of the kitchen almost every day. If that was a reason to kill someone, he'd have been dead years ago." She placed the nearly empty crystal glass on the table and patted my arm. "I wouldn't lose any sleep over it, doll."

My phone trilled and I dug it out of my purse. I looked at the caller ID. Richard. Kate and I had an appointment in half an hour to meet Richard and a bride at the rental showroom so she could select the linens and tableware for her wedding. Richard loved these meetings and could examine every cloth until he found the perfect match, whereas I lost steam after the third ivory damask.

71

"Don't tell me you're already there," I said after flipping my phone open.

"I've put together some looks and wanted to get your opinion before the bride arrives. Do you think she'll go for fuchsia and tangerine iridescent overlays?"

I swallowed a mouthful of salad. "Doesn't this bride want pastels?"

Richard groaned. "If I have to do another pastel wedding, I'm going to kill myself. You need to see these overlays, Annabelle. They're scrumptious, and they have beaded chair caps to go with them."

"You're going to try to sell her on chair caps?" I couldn't imagine my conservative bride going for covering only the top half of the chair back and dangling beads off them.

"They're the latest thing in chair accessories, Annabelle. Not quite a chair cover, but a little something to finish the look. Did I mention that they're beaded?"

"Isn't this a garden party?"

"I thought of making it more 'garden party in the Kasbah.' Do you still have that source for renting a camel?"

Now it was my turn to groan. "We'll be right there." I dropped the phone in my purse and took a final gulp of iced tea.

"Let me guess." Kate put her fork down and pulled her jacket off the back of her chair. "That was Richard."

I nodded. "He's already at the showroom, and they have new cloths. And beaded chair caps."

"Say no more." Georgia laughed. She'd tried to convince Richard to cross over to hotel catering a few years ago, but he hadn't been able to handle the concept of standard beige linens and banquet chairs. "I hope you get there before it's too late."

I shook my head. "With Richard I'd say we're way past that point."

Chapter 10

"Tell me this isn't the most delicious fabric you've ever seen." Richard opened the door to Perfect Party Rentals with swaths of shimmery orange and pink organza draped over his shoulders.

"It's like an upscale toga party," Kate whispered to me.

"Be glad it's not." I leaned into her ear. "Those are see-through overlays."

We followed him into the English basement showroom, which had been chosen precisely for its lack of windows and abundance of wall space for displays. Racks of cloths and glass shelves packed with china and crystal lined the walls of the compact space, and small tables were set up throughout the two open rooms, showing possible table vignettes. One table was designed entirely in blue with a hand-beaded turquoise cloth, blue glass base plates, and pale aqua water goblets. Next to it, celadon twill covered a table and pooled to the floor, covered with a Battenberg lace overlay and topped with white leaf plates and green and pink tulip glasses. I ran my finger over the fine gauge cotton of the Battenberg lace and sighed. I always felt decoratively challenged after visiting the rental showroom then returning to my own sparse apartment.

"Well?" Richard spun around, letting the sheer cloths flutter near his legs. "If this doesn't make a statement, I don't know what does."

"I don't think that's the statement Pam is going for." I pulled out a white chivari chair with a turquoise cushion and sat down at the blue table. The bamboo ladder-backed chivaris were my first choice for weddings for their delicate appearance, but they weren't the world's most comfortable chairs. But, as I told my clients, you don't want your guests to be so comfortable that they sit all night.

"If she wants a dull garden party, then fine." Richard rested a hand on his hip. "But at least let me give her the option of being fabulous." Richard made it sound like being fabulous was a God-given right that should be emblazoned alongside life, liberty, and the pursuit of happiness.

"Have at it. I won't stand in your way." I leveled a finger at Richard. "But no camels. If you want camels, you have to clean up after them."

Richard's mouth gaped open, then he glared at me. "Fine. We'll do without the camels." He lowered his voice. "Although they would have been perfect."

Kate joined me at the blue table. "Can I watch? I feel a nap coming on."

"You shouldn't have had lunch." Richard wagged a finger at her. "I never eat during the day. Slows me down. A Red Bull is the perfect liquid lunch."

"We only had salads at the Fairmont." Kate put her head on the table. "I think it's the wine that's making me sleepy."

Richard raised an eyebrow at us. "Aren't we fancy?"

"Don't look at me," I said. "If I had a glass of wine with lunch, I'd be asleep under the table already."

"Speaking of drinking during the day, how is Miss Rhodes?" Richard asked. "And Miss Connell?"

"O'Connell," I corrected him. "They're fine."

"Right." He smirked. "The girl with the Irish name who looks about as Irish as I do." Richard's dark hair and skin favored his Italian side of the family, though he preferred to claim only his French lineage.

"You know, Richard, not all Irish have red hair. Haven't you heard the phrase 'Black Irish'?"

Kate looked up. "That's what that means?"

Before I could make an attempt at an explanation, we heard a rap on the door behind us. Pam Monroe stuck her head inside the room and waved.

A petite girl who wore her ash blond hair swept back in a French twist, Pam taught elementary school in Georgetown and looked the part. She fell on the easygoing end of the bride spectrum, and didn't seem to have an image of the perfect wedding seared in her mind like most girls. Her fiancé, on the other hand, had made partner at one of D.C.'s largest law firms and had a clear idea of the way he wanted things. But since he was too busy to attend most of the wedding appointments, we were left to interpret his wishes. I hoped he'd be happy with our guesswork.

"Sorry I'm late." Pam came into the showroom swinging her oversized, quilted bag filled with rows of tabbed folders. I was grateful these were for her fourth grade class and not her wedding plans, although I'd had brides with wedding binders so complex that they'd required a separate index.

I stood up to greet her. "No problem. We were looking at some of the newest linens. Should we wait a few more minutes for Bill?"

Pam flushed and shook her head. "He can't make it. An important meeting came up at the last minute. You know how that goes."

We knew. An important meeting had come up when we'd gone on site visits, met with caterers, and interviewed photographers. He'd stayed at the invitation appointment long enough to veto the gorgeous letterpress invitation on handmade paper that Pam liked and to insist on traditional Crane's cards with black engraving. I, for one, wouldn't miss him.

Richard cleared his throat. "Annabelle and Kate told me that you want to have a classic garden party."

"Evermay is such a perfect place for our wedding reception," Pam explained. "The mansion is beautiful, of course, but we fell in love with the tiered gardens

76

and the fountains. Since it should still be nice weather in October, Bill and I thought it would be fun to have a jazz ensemble playing as guests wandered around. We want it to be simple and elegant."

Simple and elegant. These were words almost every bride uttered, and each meant an entirely different thing by it. I'd learned early on that what was simple and elegant to one bride was simply awful to another.

Richard clapped his hands together. "Fun you say? I'm getting a vision of something truly fun and fabulous. Envision canopies with huge lounging cushions tucked around the gardens. I'm picturing using hot pink, mango, and yellow as a modern twist on the autumn palette." He unfurled the shimmery pink and orange cloths from his arms. "Tell me this isn't to die for."

Pam rubbed the organza between her fingers. "I never thought of using bright colors. Bill usually likes white for everything. It's simpler, you know."

Kate rolled her eyes at me then turned to Pam. "I'm sure Bill will love whatever you choose. Why not have a little fun with your wedding?"

Pam smiled tentatively and eyed the fabric again. "It's a possibility."

"Or we could go with something totally different." Richard tossed the organza overlays to the side and ran to the racks of linens. He pawed through brocades until he reached a matte gold cloth. "What about an evening in Tuscany? We do lots of rich brocade cloths and use the existing stone tables in the gardens as bars.

We can have lemon topiaries and use rustic pottery for serving platters."

"That sounds nice, too. We are going to Italy on our honeymoon."

"Perfect." Richard pulled the gold brocade down and threw it over a bare table. He rushed to the other side of the room and plucked a chunky wine goblet and gold glass base plate from the wall display. "Wouldn't this be divine?"

Pam tilted her head and examined the table. "That's another possibility."

I interpreted her hesitant look. "Maybe something a bit more streamlined, Richard?"

He frowned at me then pulled a green toile cloth from the racks. "Do you have a stopover in Provence on your honeymoon, perhaps?"

"No, but that's pretty." Pam reached out and touched the linen. "It's very gardeny."

Richard threw the toile over the brocade and placed a white grape leaf plate and green glass on top. "You can't get more gardeny than green and white toile. We could use these on all the outside tables."

"Maybe, but the fabric is a little busy. There are shepherds and sheep on it."

Richard's mouth fell open. "That's the whole point of toile—"

I cut him off as I walked over to the linen racks and pulled down a pink and green plaid cloth. "Plaid is simpler, but still has a garden feel to it. Where would you put this, Richard?"

78

"Right back on the shelf where you found it." Richard made a face as he reached around me for a cloth embroidered with tiny palm trees. "I've got it! We do a British Colonial theme with everything in beige and whites. We bring in tall palms to put in the tent, or better yet, we serve the dinner entirely outside on long narrow tables."

Pam nodded. "That does sound simpler. I think Bill would like beige and white."

"We could still do some canopies outside for the cocktail hour." Richard threw the embroidered cloth over the toile and then hurried to the other side of the room for a woven rattan base plate. He placed it on the table and dabbed his forehead with a white hem-stitched napkin. "Instead of colored organza, though, we could do white panels of sheer fabric. They would flutter in the breeze and be divine."

Pam beamed at Richard. "I love the idea of dinner outside. But what about doing the tables in white, as well?"

Richard's face fell a bit, but he pulled a white crinkled fabric down and draped it on the growing stack of table linens. "Like that?"

"Possibly, but what about this?" Pam made a beeline for the cotton cloths at the far end of the wall and produced a white one. She removed the rattan plate and spread the new linen over the crinkled fabric. She pulled a white base plate and a standard issue wineglass from the display shelves to go on top.

"White twill?" A bead of sweat crept down

Richard's forehead. "You want a plain cotton table-cloth at Evermay?"

"I think it's perfect," Kate said. "It's simple yet elegant."

Richard shot daggers at her. "Are we still doing the canopies draped in fabric at least?"

"Possibly." Pam slung her tote bag on her shoulder again. "I'll have to see if Bill thinks it's too much, though. He likes things simple, you know."

Richard patted his brow. "I'm beginning to get the picture. So we're going with long tables of white twill with white plates and all-purpose glassware."

Kate fluttered her eyes at Richard. "Should I write that down for you?"

He looked at her and tapped his temple. "It's all in here."

"This was easy." Pam let out a breath, walking to the door. "Now all we have to do is pick a florist who can do simple arrangements to go with our look."

"Not a problem," I said. I already had a minimalist designer in mind.

Pam called over her shoulder. "We were thinking of all white flowers."

White flowers. Why wasn't I surprised? And how much more could we discuss about all white flowers?

Once the door shut, Richard moaned. "White, white, white, white. Remind me to wear sunglasses to this wedding."

"Come on Richard." I patted him on the shoulder. "It sounds very classic and pretty."

80

"I know." He pulled the crystal off the table and put it roughly back on the display shelf. "But the hot pink and mango tents were going to be stunning. Too bad 'Possibly Pam' is too timid to choose anything but white. I'll have to find another client to use my genius on."

"I don't think that would have fit at Evermay, anyway," Kate said. "Call me crazy, but I don't see camels at a stately Georgetown mansion."

"You have no grand vision," Richard snapped and began pulling the used linens off the display table.

My cell phone chirped, and I dug it out of my purse. "Wedding Belles. This is Annabelle." I heard muffled sobs on the other end of the phone. "Hello? Who is this?"

"It's Darcy from the Fairmont." A loud sniffle. "They took Georgia away."

"What do you mean? They fired her?" Kate and Richard stopped their bickering and looked at me.

"No," Darcy choked on a sob. "They arrested her for Henri's murder."

Chapter 11

"They can't really believe that Georgia would murder someone." Richard braced his arm against the dashboard as Kate jerked her car to a stop in front of the District Two police station. He'd whined so much about the empty Starbucks cups littering the back that

I'd relinquished the front seat to him for the short ride across town. "She would never risk breaking a nail."

I eyed the low brick building that was hidden away in a quiet neighborhood near the National Cathedral. "I don't think they took her manicure into consideration."

"And they call themselves detectives." Richard stepped out of the car and smoothed his suit jacket.

"Try to be nice, Richard." I slammed the car door behind me. "And inconspicuous."

"Maybe he should wait in the car," Kate suggested, grinning at Richard.

Richard looked pointedly at Kate's translucent blouse. "Maybe we both should."

Who needed children when I had these two? "Listen. We're here because Georgia asked us to come. Both of you behave in there, understand?"

They grumbled as they followed me up the sidewalk. I pushed through the glass double doors and approached the faux wood counter where a uniformed officer flipped through a stack of papers. A few officers sat behind him at desks that were jammed together with barely enough space between them to walk.

The officer glanced up at me from under thick black eyebrows and reached for the No Parking signs and logbook. "How many do you need this time?" His gravelly voice barely rose above the chatter of the officers behind him.

I usually came in here about once a month to get

reserved parking signs to put in front of downtown churches. That way we made sure to have at least a space or two for the bride's limousine if parking was tight. And in D.C. parking was always tight.

"I don't need any signs today, but thanks." I'd started stockpiling them in my car trunk to cut down on trips to the station. "I'm actually here to see someone you've arrested."

One of his bushy brows rose up at the corner. "Name?"

"I'm Annabelle Archer." I turned to motion behind me. "This is my assistant, Kate—"

The officer cleared his throat to interrupt me. "Not your name. The name of the person you're here to see."

"Georgia Rhodes." My face flushed with embarrassment as the officers behind him looked up and snickered. I hoped I had plenty of signs in my car because I wouldn't be coming back here for a while.

"Are you family?"

This wasn't going well. Kate stepped forward and leaned on the desk. "Can't you tell that they're sisters?"

The officer pulled his gaze away from Kate's blouse and studied me for a second. "Not really."

"Her sister dyes her hair," Kate confided to the cop. "She's not really blond."

"I thought she looked like a bottle job." The officer returned Kate's smile. I crossed my fingers that Georgia wasn't within earshot. "Let me check and see if she's allowed to have visitors." He left the desk and disappeared into the back offices.

"Nice going, Kate," I whispered. "What if they figure out I'm not related to Georgia?"

"Impossible. How could they prove that? You could be her half sister or her stepsister. There are lots of reasons you wouldn't have the same last name."

"Or look even remotely alike?"

Kate shrugged. "Recessive genes."

"What if Georgia tells them she doesn't have a sister?" Richard tapped his foot on the worn linoleum floor behind us.

I narrowed my eyes at Kate. "Well?"

Her cheeks flushed. "I never thought of that. I guess then you'd have some explaining to do."

Richard took a step toward the door. "Maybe we should leave before they find out that Annabelle lied about being Georgia's sister. This place gives me the heebie-jeebies, anyway."

"I'm with Richard." Kate backed away from the counter, her face now a bright pink. "Annabelle could get in big trouble for messing with an investigation."

"Might I remind you that you lied to the officer?" I managed to say even though my mouth had gone completely dry. I wondered if the officer would chase us if we made a run for it. Too late. He was approaching the counter.

"It's okay for you to see her." He pointed a finger at me. "But only you. Your friends will have to wait here."

I turned to say something to Kate and Richard, but they were already at the glass entrance doors.

"We'll wait in the car." Kate waved with her keys as Richard held the door open. "Take your time."

I mouthed the word "cowards" to them as I followed the stocky cop behind the counter. He led me to a room with several brown chairs clustered around a wooden table. Georgia sat in one of the chairs with her legs tightly crossed. The officer held the door as I went inside, then closed it behind me.

Georgia looked up and a smile broke across her face. "Thank God you're here."

I leaned in for an air kiss. "How are you doing?"

"I'm sitting in a pleather chair in a police station. How do you think I'm doing?"

"Don't worry, Georgia." I eyed the fake leather chairs with strips of duct tape patching the edges as I took a seat across from her. "This has to be a mistake. They can't really believe that you would kill Henri. What evidence do they have aside from the fact that you hated him and don't have an alibi?"

She shook her head. "There can't be any evidence. I was nowhere near the murder scene. Like I told you, I was in my office doing those damn reports all day."

"But no one saw you?"

"Everyone else was working the wedding. Since Darcy had to do my job of coordinating the setup, I didn't even see her for hours." She tapped a pink, perfectly polished nail on the table. "I'm sure they won't waste any time giving her my position now."

"First of all, I don't think Darcy wants your job. She doesn't like dealing with clients, remember?"

"It doesn't matter. The general manager would love to toss me out and put in someone who won't outshine him." Her eyes glimmered with tears. "What am I going to do?"

I reached out and squeezed her hand. "Everything will be fine. The police can't have any evidence to prosecute you with, and the GM can't fire you just because everyone likes you more than him."

Georgia put a hand over her eyes. "You don't understand. The hotel is my life. I've worked almost every weekend for eight years so other people can have amazing parties. I can't remember the last time I had a steady boyfriend. And I'm going to lose it all."

"You're not going to lose everything. Anyway, there are lots of other jobs."

She gaped at me. "Start over? Do you know how hard it would be to get hired in another luxury hotel after being fired, not to mention arrested for murder?" A tear snaked down her cheek. "Do you know how many weddings I've done at the hotel? How many brides I've watched go down the aisle? I've given up a normal life for this career, and I have absolutely nothing to show for it. No wedding of my own, no kids, no house in the burbs, nothing." Her shoulders began to shake, and she buried her face in her hands.

My jaw hit the floor. Georgia's life seemed so glamorous to me. Beautiful clothes, perfect hair, a chic downtown apartment. Even in college she'd been the golden girl with the cute boyfriend and even cuter clothes. I'd always aspired to what I'd thought was Georgia's life of champagne and caviar. Who would've guessed that she wanted 2.5 kids and a house with a picket fence? "I had no idea. . . ."

"Be careful, Annabelle," she said through sobs. "In this business, you snap your fingers and a decade has gone by."

Tears pricked the back of my eyes as I watched her cry. I swallowed hard and tried to sound upbeat. "It's not the end of the world. This will all blow over and you'll be back at the hotel in no time."

She looked up at me. Tears had muddied the smoky shadow on her eyes, and she wiped dark streaks with the back of her hand. "Will you help me, Annabelle? I can't trust anyone at the hotel anymore, and you've been such a good friend. You remind me of myself when I first started in this industry."

I wasn't sure that was such a compliment now that I had a firsthand look at where years of planning events got you, but I owed it to Georgia after all she'd done for me. "Of course. What do you want me to do?"

She leaned forward and lowered her voice. "No one at the hotel will tell the police anything, but they might talk to you. People there know you. They like you. Could you ask around? Try to find out any gossip that might help clear me. The real killer must be someone in the hotel, and someone has to have seen or heard something."

That sounded simple enough. No danger in eavesdropping. "Don't worry. We'll find out who really killed Henri and get you out of here." I looked at Georgia's swollen, red-rimmed eyes and took both of her hands firmly in mine. I tried to sound more confident than I felt. "I promise."

"Time's up, ma'am." The stout officer stood at the door.

I gave Georgia's hands one more squeeze before I followed the cop back out to the entrance. Three men stood talking in front of the glass doors, and I recognized the man in a snug-fitting blue polo shirt. Detective Reese. Great. I put my head down and tried to scoot around the group so he wouldn't notice me and accuse me of meddling in another investigation.

"Miss Archer?"

Crap. He noticed me. I looked up and flashed him a quick grin but didn't stop walking.

"Hold up a second."

I pivoted around and tried not to let the panic I felt creep into my voice. "Hi, Detective."

He took a step to close the distance between us. "What are you doing here?"

I blurted out the first thing I could think of. "I'm picking up some No Parking signs for a wedding."

He looked at my empty hands and raised an eyebrow. "Really? Where are they?"

I dropped my eyes to my hands. No signs. Nice going, Annabelle. I opened my mouth to explain, and then thought better of making up another lie. I wished I had Kate's ability to flirt her way out of any situation, even though she credited the Wonder Bra for a great deal of her success. It would take the mother of all Wonder Bras to get me out of this one.

Reese took me by the arm and leaned close to me. "Does this have anything to do with the arrest we made in the chef's murder? I would have thought you'd steer clear of the case now that you're no longer a suspect."

I tried to pull away, but he held my arm tight against him. "You were mistaken when you suspected me, and you're mistaken about Georgia, too."

"Please tell me this woman isn't a friend of yours." Reese rolled his eyes as he released me.

"I've known her for years, and I can tell you for a fact that she could never murder anyone," I insisted. "Even Henri."

Reese grinned at me, his hazel eyes deepening to green. "You sure know how to pick 'em, sweetheart. She's as guilty as they come."

My cheeks burned. Now I remembered how cocky he was. "Just because she doesn't have an alibi? You're pinning it on her because you haven't found the real killer."

Reese's smile vanished. "We have evidence that links her to the crime scene. The fact that she doesn't have an alibi is icing on the cake."

"What evidence? I was at the crime scene, remember?"

"How could I forget?" He gave me an exasperated sigh. "We found an item belonging to Miss Rhodes with traces of the chef's blood on it. Unfortunately the media got wind of it, too, so you can read all about it in tomorrow's paper."

"What item?" This sounded suspicious. I'd heard about police planting evidence. "How can you be sure it belongs to her?"

"Apparently Miss Rhodes has a scarf that she wears frequently. It's been called her 'signature' scarf by several coworkers. We found it wedged in the back of her desk drawer with drops of dried blood on it."

Georgia's Jackie O Hermès scarf? My heart sank. She idolized Jackie almost as much as she did Marilyn, and the scarf was one of her prized possessions.

"I'm afraid it doesn't look good for your friend." Reese shook his head.

I was afraid he was right.

Chapter 12

"You still think she's innocent?" Kate handed her keys to the Fairmont Hotel valet the next morning. We'd made record time from my apartment to the hotel after she picked me up. "They found blood on her Jackie O scarf."

"Of course I believe she's innocent." I stepped out of the car and smoothed out the wrinkles in my blue pencil skirt. Even though Detective Reese had momentarily shaken my belief in Georgia's innocence, I was still determined to help her. "Someone set

90

her up. Someone who wants her out of the way."

Kate came around the back of her car, tucking a white shirt into black boot-cut pants that left little to the imagination. "Who?"

"That's what we're here to find out." I'd convinced Kate to join me in a little hotel reconnaissance on Georgia's behalf only after I threatened to turn the Egan wedding over to her. Our office code name for Hillary Egan was "Hillary Again" because she called ten times a day and her wedding was still seven months away.

I led the way into the lobby of the hotel and made a beeline for the concierge desk when I saw that Hugh was on duty. He looked every bit the proper concierge, standing ramrod straight in his dark blue jacket and gold concierge pin. Despite his formal appearance, he served as D.C.'s command center for gossip. He knew everything that went on in the hotel and the city. The fact that he didn't mind sharing his information made him my favorite concierge.

He smiled when he saw us and held up a finger as he finished making dinner reservations for a guest. When he hung up the phone, he glanced around him. "What are you two doing back here? Run. Save yourselves."

Kate laughed. "That bad?"

"It's like being on the *Titanic*," he muttered, smoothing his tidy brown moustache with one finger. "We're down two people in three days."

"You haven't lost Georgia for good." I tried to sound more confident than I felt. "Once the police realize they've made a mistake by arresting her, I'm sure she'll be back to work."

Hugh gave a quick shake of his head. "I doubt it. The general manager isn't thrilled about having one of his catering sales staff arrested for murdering his head chef."

"But if they find out she's innocent, they have to give her back her job," I insisted.

"They can find a hundred ways to fire her. If Mr. Elliott wants her gone, she'll be gone." Hugh slid a map across to me. "This makes it look like I'm working."

I took the map and flipped it open. "Do you think Georgia killed Henri?"

Hugh fingered the gold concierge pin on his lapel and thought for a moment. "No. She has a bit of a temper, but I wouldn't peg her as the violent type."

Kate put an arm up on the marble countertop. "Annabelle thinks she was framed."

Hugh's eyes widened and he looked positively giddy. "Really? Who do you think framed her?"

"That's where we thought you could help out. You must know who would want to get rid of Georgia." I leaned in for the kill. "You know everything."

Hugh blushed. "Not everything. I mean I do know a lot about what goes on here. Most of it is who's having an affair or who got drunk and made a fool of themself. That kind of thing. Not who's setting up someone else to take a murder rap."

"Forget the murder, then," Kate whispered. "Tell us the juicy stuff."

I frowned at her. "We're not here for random gossip, Kate." Kate made a face at me.

"I can tell you that Georgia wasn't always the most popular girl in the hotel," Hugh said in a lowered voice as two hotel guests passed us. "The banquet captains complained that she changed her room diagrams at the last minute, and Mr. Elliott had to chase down her paperwork."

"Those don't sound like reasons to frame someone for murder," I said.

"You're right," Hugh admitted. "As much as we all despise Mr. Elliott, I doubt he'd frame someone for murder. He's too spineless to do something like that. I'm sure that Georgia's arrest is a lucky break for him. He'd been searching for a way to get rid of her without looking like the bad guy. And as much as Georgia drove them crazy with last minute changes, the banquet staff really is fond of her. She could make you insane and make you love her at the same time."

I looked pointedly at Kate. "I know the feeling."

"Back to the drawing board." Kate ignored me, squinting at something across the lobby.

I followed her gaze and did a double take. "Is that Ian?"

"Who?" Kate turned back to me, confused. "I didn't notice his face. I only got as far up as his jeans, which he wears very well."

"The bandleader from Saturday." As I watched Ian deep in a conversation with what looked like a hotel cook, I pulled my ponytail holder out and my hair fell loose down my back. "I wonder why he's here again. And who is he talking to?"

"He used to bartend in the hotel and returns to say hi every so often. The guy he's talking to is Emilio, one of the sous chefs." Hugh grinned at me. "What I'm curious about is why you let your hair down."

"What?" I put a hand through my hair. I knew I looked better with it down, even if I rarely wore it that way. "I got tired of it being up, that's all."

Kate folded her arms across her chest. "I do believe you're flustered, Annabelle."

"Don't be absurd. I'm not flustered," I lied. "I'm confused that he never mentioned working here before. He made it sound like he didn't know Chef Henri."

Hugh groaned. "Everyone who worked here during the past ten years knew Henri. None of us were spared."

Kate nudged me with her elbow. "I think he's spotted you, Annabelle. He's coming this way."

Ian wore a white T-shirt that covered most of the tattoos on his biceps, but I caught myself staring at the hard curves of his arms anyway. I tried to smile as naturally as possible with Kate snickering behind me.

"We meet again." Ian kissed my hand and then Kate's, and nodded at Hugh. "You know I have a weakness for redheads."

"I do now." Hugh arched an eyebrow at me, and I could bet that it would be a matter of minutes before the entire city heard the story.

Ian met my eyes with his own blue ones. "And long red hair, too." He winked at me. "I knew you would be trouble the moment I saw you."

"What are you doing here?" I stammered. Not my most eloquent moment.

His eyes flitted to Hugh, then back to me. "The lads left a power cord the other night so I'm picking it up. Lucky for me I ran into you. Wouldn't you call this fate?"

"I don't know." I looked back to Kate for help, but she just smiled at me. For once it seemed like she didn't mind sharing the spotlight. Of course, I knew she'd be teasing me about this for years to come.

"What are you doing on Friday night?" he asked.

My mind blanked for a moment. "I have a rehearsal for a wedding."

"All night?"

"No, but after that I should get ready—"

"Good. Plan on dinner with me, then. You have to eat, don't you?" He kissed me quickly on the cheek and left with a wave to Kate and Hugh before I could say a word. The light scent of his cologne lingered on me, and I inhaled deeply as he walked out the glass doors of the hotel. Kate had been right about his jeans. He looked awfully good in them.

Kate gave a low whistle. "That was impressive."

I raised an unsteady hand to where he'd kissed my cheek. "I think I have a date."

Kate wore a look of admiration. "That guy is smooth. You definitely have a date."

Hugh let out a breath. "I think *my* knees are weak."

"I think I'm going to throw up." I hadn't had a real date in so long, the thought of one nearly brought on a panic attack.

"Don't worry." Kate threw an arm around my shoulders. "I'll bring you up to speed and give you some tips."

I laughed. "Now I'm really scared."

"It's about time you had a little fun. D.C. women focus too much on their careers," Hugh said, then gave a small wave to someone behind me. "Speaking of all work and no play . . ."

I turned as Darcy walked up, taking short fast steps, her long dark hair swinging behind her. She pushed her glasses up onto the top of her head and rubbed her temples. Her eyes were bloodshot and had dark circles underneath.

"Have you come to help?" She slumped against the concierge desk.

Kate stared at her. "What happened to you? You look awful." Leave it to Kate to be subtle.

"You try doing the work of two people," Darcy complained. "It's impossible to keep up."

"Kate doesn't even do the work of one person." I sidestepped as Kate swatted at me.

Darcy managed a weak smile, and then wrinkled her brow. "Do you guys need anything from catering? Please tell me you aren't one of the twenty proposals that Georgia left in her inbox. And I've only gotten halfway through returning all her messages."

"No, we only came by to find information to help clear Georgia," I said. "We promised her we'd try to help." From the look of things, Georgia didn't need to worry about Darcy wanting her job.

"Yes, please! Did you see her?" Darcy's eyes widened. "They wouldn't let me in because I'm not family."

I nodded. "She swears that she didn't kill Henri, and she thinks someone is setting her up."

Darcy looked at Hugh. "Who would want her gone bad enough to do that?"

Hugh shrugged. "My only guesses were Mr. Elliott or one of the captains."

Darcy frowned. "Not the captains. They're all bark. Mr. Elliott would love any excuse to fire her, but I can't imagine him being involved in a murder. He's more the type to wait for someone to hang themselves."

"Sounds charming," Kate said.

Hugh leaned over the counter. "Does Mr. Elliott know about the fight?"

Darcy leveled a finger at him. "No, and if you tell anyone . . ."

"You know I would never spread rumors that would get Georgia in trouble." Hugh recoiled at the accusation.

"What fight?" Kate asked.

"This is just between us, right?" Darcy motioned for us to come closer. "No one knows about this except for Hugh. If the police or Mr. Elliott found out,

97

Georgia would be done for."

Kate made a zipper motion across her lips. "You can trust us."

Darcy took a deep breath. "Henri came up to Georgia's office. He was steamed about the pricing of a menu she'd done. I didn't hear most of it because they closed the door, but when he opened the door to leave, I heard him threatening to tell Mr. Elliott that Georgia had no idea how to do her job. Georgia yelled back that she wished he was dead and threw a glass paperweight from her desk at him."

Kate sucked in air. "Did she hit him?"

"She missed and hit the wall instead," Darcy continued. "Henri stormed out."

I gulped. "You didn't tell the police?"

Darcy reddened. "I guess maybe I should have, but I know Georgia didn't kill him. She didn't really mean what she said. It was the heat of the moment. We've all joked about wishing Henri was dead. I knew if I told the police, it would look bad for Georgia."

"When was the fight?" I asked.

Darcy cringed. "The morning of the wedding."

Kate put a hand to her mouth. "The same day Henri was murdered?"

Darcy nodded. She was right. Georgia had motive, evidence linking her to the victim, and no alibi. It looked very bad indeed.

Chapter 13

"You look like you need a drink, darling." Richard perched on the edge of an upholstered bench as Kate and I collapsed onto the beige sofa in his office sitting room. The couch was a sleek, modern design, more angles than cushion, and my back immediately regretted the choice.

I shifted around, trying to get comfortable. "I wish. Isn't a bride meeting us here, though?"

"Viola Van de Kamp and her mother, Louise." Richard looked at his watch. Ever since he'd gotten a Cartier, he checked the time with a regularity that bordered on compulsive. "They're three minutes late."

"That name sounds familiar." A little red light went off faintly in the back of my brain, but my mind swirled with questions about Georgia and her connection to Chef Henri's death. Was it a coincidence that Henri died only hours after he so enraged Georgia that she threw a paperweight at him? If Georgia was on the verge of being fired, would she do something desperate to keep Henri from threatening her job?

Richard cleared his throat. "So you girls have been out and about already today?"

Kate leaned her head back against the back of the sofa. "Annie wanted to poke around at the Fairmont. Ask a few questions about Georgia."

"Any luck?" Richard looked back and forth between us.

"No," I confessed. "We actually found out that Georgia had an incriminating fight with Henri the day of the murder. She screamed that she wished he was dead and hurled a paperweight at him."

"She missed, though," Kate added.

"Heaven help us." Richard rolled his eyes. "Now I like Georgia as much as anyone, but do you really think you can find anything that will convince the police she's innocent?"

"If I don't help her, who will? She's all alone and about to lose everything." I felt my jaw tighten. "I know she'd do the same thing for me."

Richard put up his hands. "Okay, okay. Just asking. Personally, I think she should plead temporary insanity. Anyone who gets blood on an Hermès scarf has clearly lost her mind. I'd acquit her in a second."

I laughed despite my best efforts not to. "Very funny. But she didn't get blood on the scarf. She was framed."

"You don't say? Who framed her?"

Kate leaned forward and cupped a hand around her mouth. "We're still working on that minor detail."

"You can make all the jokes you want, Richard, but we're going to find out who really killed Henri and set Georgia up."

"As long as you do it after we meet with the Van de Kamps." Richard stood up and unbuttoned the bottom button on his black suit jacket. He never liked his jackets buttoned all the way because he claimed it looked too uptight. "They're interested in wedding planners, not a crime fighting duo. And they haven't signed my contract yet, so a few mentions about how fabulous I am would be appreciated."

"You're sure these are good clients, right?" I asked. "Not a bride who thinks that decorating the reception with origami is a good idea?"

Richard put a hand on his hip. "You're still steamed about that, aren't you?"

"I can make paper cranes in my sleep," Kate complained.

"This is a Potomac family who wants to throw a big bash for their only daughter. I guarantee you won't be doing arts and crafts for them." Richard jumped as the doorbell rang.

The door opened and I heard footsteps in the foyer. Richard rushed forward to greet them, but all I could see as Mrs. Van de Kamp rounded the corner was blue eye shadow and lots of it. It took me only a second to recognize the girl in the shapeless dress behind her mother. I looked at Kate, whose eyes widened in recognition and fear.

It was Viola the Vegan.

"Weren't you two at the bridal tea?" Viola eyed us warily. She looked less than thrilled to be there, and I had a feeling there had been some sort of coercion involved.

"You must be Mrs. Van de Kamp." I stepped forward and took the mother's hand. I turned to Viola and forced a smile. "And you must be the bride."

Viola barely took my hand. "You must be a genius."

Kate and I exchanged glances. The last thing we needed was to deal with Bratty Bride for the next year. Richard laughed nervously and motioned for us to sit down.

I took my seat on the couch. I avoided looking at Richard for fear I might be overcome with the need to bludgeon him to death. "Tell us about your wedding plans so far."

"Isn't that why we'd hire you?" Viola slouched down in an armchair. "To plan the wedding?"

I liked this girl less every second. The faster I could get out of this, the better. I turned to the mother. "Have you set a date?"

"We're looking at next fall, but we want to see what your availability is before settling on a day." Mrs. Van de Kamp sounded desperate, and I could see why. "You come highly recommended from Richard."

So much for saying we were already booked, if she intended to plan the wedding around our availability. Leaving the country to get out of it seemed a bit extreme.

"I need to get married before Jupiter goes retrograde, Mother." Viola gave an exasperated sigh. "So it has to be before October seventeenth."

Then again, maybe relocating the business overseas wasn't such an outrageous plan.

"Come again?" Kate did little to hide her curiosity.

Viola rolled her eyes as if we were idiots for not knowing the star charts. "After Jupiter goes into retrograde, it won't be good for me to enter into any unions. That includes marriage."

"Absolute nonsense," her mother snapped. "I will not rearrange a wedding based on what a telephone astrologer told you."

Viola crossed her arms in front of her. "Fine. Then I won't come."

Richard jumped up and rushed to the wooden sideboard by the window. "I forgot to offer everyone some champagne. We always start off the wedding planning with a toast."

This was new. I suspected Richard had made it up to force everyone to have a drink and loosen up. Not a bad plan.

"Why don't we worry about the date later and talk about general style," I said as Richard briskly tore the foil off a champagne bottle. "What's your vision of the wedding?"

"I want an outdoor ceremony," Viola started before her mother could speak. "Something very rustic. No formal gardens. And I want to use lots of seasonal flowers and leaves."

Okay. Not a bad start. An outdoor, autumn wedding could be beautiful. Maybe this wouldn't be a disaster after all.

"What colors were you thinking for bridesmaids?" Kate asked.

"They're going to be called wood nymphs, not bridesmaids, and I thought they could be in body stockings with leaves sewn on."

I bit my lip to keep from laughing. This would be

103

one bridesmaid—oops, wood nymph—outfit that no one could ever claim to wear again.

Mrs. Van de Kamp gave a muffled cry. "You can't make your friends wear leaf pasties to your wedding."

"Bridesmaids dresses are stupid." Viola squared her shoulders. "So are bouquets. I want them to carry floral tambourines instead."

Now this I wanted to see. Although I doubted she'd have any friends left after she told them they were wearing leotards and shaking tambourines down the aisle. I could see Kate begin to tremble with silent laughter next to me.

"Champagne anyone?" Richard rushed over with a round metal tray of crystal champagne flutes.

Mrs. Van de Kamp took a glass and downed it in one gulp. Even under her tire track blush, I could see her cheeks burn with anger. I didn't blame her.

"Is it sulfite free?" Viola gave the tray a suspicious glance.

"No." Richard spun on his heel away from her. "Better not have any."

"I think we should do this at a later date, once Viola has had an opportunity to rethink her ideas." Mrs. Van de Kamp stood and jerked Viola up by the sleeve. "Thank you, ladies. Richard." She pulled the girl all the way across the room and out the door as Kate and I hurried to stand up. The door slammed behind them.

Richard held the tray of champagne in one hand and downed glass after glass with the other. "What the hell was that?"

"Exactly my question." Kate turned to him, her mouth hanging open. "You call those clients normal?"

Richard hiccuped. "I might have misjudged."

"Might?" Kate and I said in unison.

"Okay," Richard admitted. "They're awful. Can I make it up to you with dinner?"

"This one is going to cost you." Kate walked over and snatched the last glass of champagne off the tray before he could. "I'm in the mood for a French martini at Mie N Yu."

Richard put the tray down. "Shall we end the workday early and try to snag the loft table?"

"Let me run to the ladies' room while you call ahead," I said over my shoulder as I walked down the back hall. I paused outside the doors to the bathroom and kitchen, which were side by side. Whose voice was that? I stepped closer to the swinging kitchen door and pressed on it enough so it opened a fraction of an inch.

"I owe you a debt of gratitude for what you did." Marcello spoke in hushed tones. "We all do."

Why the secrecy and whispering? I leaned forward so I could see through the sliver of an opening. Marcello stood to the side holding a cordless phone.

"After all these years, he got what he deserved." Marcello gave a soft chuckle. "Finally, his career was the one put on ice."

Ice? I straightened up with a jerk. Could he be talking about Henri? Who else?

"I only wish I could have seen the look on his face," Marcello added.

I pressed against the door to see more clearly, and the hinge creaked.

Marcello froze. "Hold on a second. I think I heard something."

With my heart pounding, I let the door go and spun around. I ran back to the front of the house, passing Kate and Richard in the sitting room. I kept running to the foyer, motioning them to follow me.

"Wait for us," Kate cried, grabbing both of our purses.

Richard stood holding an empty glass of champagne as Kate hurried away. "What's the rush? They're holding the table for us."

"Come on." I gave a nervous glance toward the kitchen door. "I'll tell you once we're out of here. It's about Henri's murder."

Richard's shoulders sagged. "Again?"

I nodded. "A suspect just moved to the front of the line."

Chapter 14

"Coy does not become you, Annabelle." Richard stepped out of his convertible after parking next to us in the Georgetown lot. We'd taken separate cars to the restaurant so we wouldn't have to drive Richard back to Capitol Hill after dinner. It was early enough that we'd found space in the tiny public lot next to Mie N Yu.

"I'm not being coy. I just want to wait until we're sitting in the restaurant to tell you. Someone could overhear us on the street."

"Who?" Richard looked around us. "A homeless person or a Hari Krishna?"

"Less talking, more walking." Kate passed us and strode down the sidewalk toward the brick red and gold facade of the restaurant with sheer yellow curtains fluttering in the doorway. "I'm dying for a martini."

"You shameless hussy."

I recognized Fern's voice immediately. Or maybe it was his vocabulary I recognized. Who else called people hussies to their face? I turned to find him standing behind us wearing a long black Nehru jacket with an ornate silver cross hanging down the front. If I didn't know better, I'd have pegged him for a priest. Although the slicked back ponytail and giant rings on his fingers were a bit of a giveaway.

Kate spun around with a smirk on her face. "Look who's talking."

"I am a man of the cloth." He looked wounded, then grinned at us. "You wouldn't believe how nice people are to you when you're a priest."

Richard shook his head. "You do know you're not really a priest, right?"

"I'm a hairdresser. It's close enough," Fern explained. "I take confessions exactly like they do."

Richard frowned. "But priests don't spread the stories they hear all over town."

"A technicality, I'm sure." Fern dismissed Richard with a wave of his hands. "What I want to know is why you're tying one on at five-thirty? Isn't it a little early?"

"Not after the meeting we just had." Kate sighed. "A nightmare bride."

Fern's face lit up. "Worse than the one who had me put three tiaras in her weave? Do tell."

I looked at Richard, who shrugged his shoulders, and then I turned to Fern. "Would you like to join us for dinner?"

"Only if I wouldn't be imposing," Fern said as he linked arms with Kate and led the way into Mie N Yu without a backward glance.

As I followed them through the opening in the restaurant doorway's sheer curtains, my eyes took a few seconds to adjust to the low lighting inside. Mie N Yu had been designed around the travels of Marco Polo, so there were tons of low tables surrounded by luxurious cushions, tables perched high in cages, and red fabric cascading from the ceiling. Kind of an East meets West meets Kama Sutra. It was also a place where the pretty people of Georgetown came out to play.

After a delay appropriate for one of the city's hot spots, an aloof hostess led us to a table nestled on the landing between the first and second floors and draped with white netting. The table jutted out over the first floor and had carved wooden sides to keep people from falling over. This was the perfect place for talking without being overheard since there were no other tables near us. Kate and Fern began studying the martini menu immediately.

"Well, are you going to tell us now?" Richard tapped his fingers on the round wooden table.

I waited until the hostess had descended the stairs again. "I overheard someone talking to Henri's killer. They were on the phone." I hesitated to implicate Richard's chef. Knowing Richard, he wouldn't take it well.

Kate pulled her eyes away from the long list of martinis. "How could you know that Henri's killer was on the other end?"

"Because they were talking about icing careers," I said patiently. "The person on my end thanked the other person for getting rid of someone they both hated."

"Enough already," Richard said with a sigh. "Who did you overhear?"

I cringed, knowing Richard wouldn't like this one bit. "Marcello. He was on the phone back at your office."

"You can't know that he was talking about Henri," Richard sputtered. "Talk about putting words in his mouth. Just because he has a past with the victim doesn't mean he's on a murder phone tree."

"It may not sound convincing, but you should have heard him," I cried. "He sounded very secretive and sinister."

"I don't think you can prosecute someone for

murder because they sound creepy on the phone." Kate looked as skeptical as Richard.

Fern waved a cute waiter over to take the drink order. "Two French martinis and . . . Annie, what are you drinking?"

"A Coke." I turned to Richard. "You said that Marcello was with you at the time of the murder, right?"

"Campari and soda for me." Richard flipped open the laminated menu and nodded. "He was the chef at our wedding at Dumbarton House."

"Give us a few more minutes to look at the menus," Fern said quietly to the waiter.

"Of course, Father." The young man gave a bow of the head as he left the table.

Richard gave Fern a look. "You're out of your mind."

"What?" Fern gave an innocent shrug. "Did I say I was a priest?"

"What if he didn't kill Henri, but had someone do the dirty work for him?" I asked, trying to steer the conversation back to the murder. "I'll bet he knows all the chefs in town."

Richard shook his head. "Why would someone commit murder for him? That seems like a pretty big favor to ask. Don't forget that Marcello was out of the industry for a while. I don't know how much he would have stayed in touch with his old colleagues."

I swiveled around on my cushioned chair. "What do you mean he was out of the industry? I thought you hired him after he left the hotel side."

110

"Henri didn't only get him fired," Richard explained. "Marcello was blackballed for years. No one would hire him. He went into a tailspin. His wife left him. He lost custody of his daughter. He basically lost everything before I took a chance on him. It was the best hiring decision I ever made, of course. The man is a culinary genius."

I swallowed hard. "That's an awful story. I had no idea." I almost didn't blame Marcello if he wanted to kill Henri. I didn't want Georgia to take the fall for it, though.

"It had to be someone on the inside to get to Henri without being noticed." Richard snapped his menu shut. "Marcello doesn't have the friends in the hotel world that he used to. I doubt he could have done it even if he wanted to."

"That makes perfect sense," Kate said as our drinks arrived. She balanced her martini gingerly as she took a sip from the flared edge. "So many people in the hotel hated Henri that it seems silly to consider suspects who would have had to come from the outside without being noticed. I think people at the Fairmont would have noticed someone as big as Marcello poking around and trying to get someone to commit murder for him."

"Maybe I should tell the police what I overheard just to be on the safe side. Even if Marcello is innocent, he might be able to lead them to the killer because he knows so many cooks who hated Henri."

Kate lowered her drink to the table. "It's true that

birds of a feather flock to leather."

Fern giggled. "My kind of birds."

Richard rolled his eyes. "This is ridiculous. You're going to tell the police that you overheard my head chef talking to an unknown person about something that may or may not be connected to a murder? Are you trying to ruin me? And are you sure you don't have an ulterior motive?"

"I don't know what you mean," I said dismissing his accusation.

"I do." Kate waved her hand in the air. "You mean Reese?"

Fern's eyes bounced back between Kate and Richard. "Who's Reese?"

"A cute detective that Annie had a crush on a while back," Kate said.

Fern bounced up and down on his chair. "I remember him. He was more than cute."

"I didn't have a crush on him," I protested. "We were strictly professional."

"I know," Kate groaned. "Such a disappointment. Leatrice had practically picked out the wedding invitations."

"Didn't he have dark hair and nice arms?" Fern raised an eyebrow.

Kate looked surprised. "Good memory. I'm impressed."

Fern pointed to the room below us. "Isn't that him over there?"

We all followed Fern's gaze to a table across the

room. Sure enough, Reese was sitting at a low table leaning up against some beaded cushions. He wore a black knit shirt that pulled tight across his chest and showed off his tan arms. My pulse quickened until I looked across from him, then my body went cold.

If she was a day over twenty-one, I'd have been shocked. Her long hair had been streaked blond, and she wore too much makeup and not nearly enough skirt.

"Maybe she's his sister." Kate turned back around with a stricken look on her face.

"I hope not." Fern hadn't taken his eyes off the couple. "I don't think it's appropriate to touch your sister on the leg like that. Even here."

"I never thought he was good enough for you, anyway." Richard made a face. "If those are the type of bimbos he likes, then good riddance. You need someone with more sophistication and polish."

"I wouldn't tell Richard about your date with Ian, then," Kate whispered to me behind her hand.

"Can you believe that outfit?" Fern shuddered. "Who would wear a skirt that short?"

"Hey," Kate cried. "I own that skirt."

Fern patted her on the hand. "And I'm sure on you it looks lovely, but right now we're trashing Annabelle's competition."

"Thanks, guys." I steadied my voice. "I'm telling you, though. I don't have a thing for Detective Reese."

Richard was right. If these were the type of women Reese liked, then I could forget about him. I could

113

never compete with Miss Legs. Girls like that didn't work sixty hour weeks and run around setting up weddings for twelve hours at a time. I reached over, took Kate's martini out of her hand and took a long drink.

"Are you still overcome with the urge to tell the police what you heard Marcello saying?" Richard asked after I returned the glass to a startled Kate.

"Let Reese figure it out on his own if he's such a great detective. He doesn't want our help, anyway." I beckoned the waiter over so I could order a martini of my own. "I'm trying to clear Georgia. The police are on their own."

After I'd ordered a French martini, Fern pulled the waiter down by the sleeve. "Give it wings, my son."

Chapter 15

"I've been waiting up for you, dearie." Leatrice stuck her head out of her first-floor apartment as I started up the stairs. "Do you want to watch an episode of *Perry Mason* with me? I found a channel that plays them late at night."

Just when I thought my social life couldn't get worse.

"I'm pretty tired, Leatrice. Kate and I were running around all day. Maybe some other time."

Leatrice pulled her door closed and followed me up the staircase. She wore a black apron that looked like the front of a tuxedo jacket complete with bow tie and ruffled shirt. It gave a whole new meaning to the phrase "black tie optional." "I heard that they arrested someone for the chef's murder."

I paused at the first landing and leaned against the metal banister. "Was it in the paper already?"

Leatrice shrugged. "I don't read the paper. Too much politics for my taste. I heard it on the scanner."

"Right." How could I forget her scanner? I eyed her apron and tried to change the subject. "So, doing some cooking?"

"Cooking?" She cocked an eyebrow at me and shook her head.

Silly me. I should have known better than to assume anything about Leatrice's choice of wardrobe. I should have been grateful she had clothes on underneath the apron. "Never mind."

"Do you know the girl they arrested?" Leatrice hurried up behind me as I took the stairs two at a time.

"She's a friend of mine and she didn't do it." I reached my doorway a bit out of breath and paused before I put the key in the lock. I thought for a second about how I could go inside without letting Leatrice in, then realized it would be impossible and opened the door anyway.

Leatrice led the way into my living room, bouncing on her toes. It was almost scary how excited she got about crime investigation. "They arrested the wrong person?"

"Definitely." I kicked off my low black pumps and

dropped my purse on the floor beside the couch. "Someone framed her for the murder."

"How do you know?" Leatrice's eyes grew wide as she sunk into the overstuffed armchair.

"Georgia isn't a killer," I said firmly. "There are lots of other people who had motive to kill the chef, as well. Better motives."

"Like who?"

"Richard's head chef, Marcello, for one." I moved a pile of papers on the couch so I could sit. "Henri ruined his life by blackballing him from the industry over ten years ago."

Leatrice edged forward in the chair so her feet touched the floor. "That's a long time to plan revenge."

"He's Italian," I explained. "From what I hear, any of the chefs who worked with Henri had strong motive to kill him."

"And you think one of them committed murder and framed your friend for it?"

"That's where I get a little fuzzy," I admitted. "The chefs have the strongest motives, but I don't know why they would want to frame Georgia. The people who would want to get Georgia out of the way—like the hotel's general manager—don't have much of a motive for killing Henri."

"That does present a problem, dear." Leatrice furrowed her brow in concentration. "It's a shame we don't have pictures of the event to search through for possible clues."

"The photographers had barely arrived at the hotel by the time we found the body," I said, then snapped my fingers and began looking around the room. "But the videographer got there early and shot footage of the courtyard."

"Was that where you found the body?" Leatrice stood up and started looking with me.

"No, but the courtyard is right outside the room where the chef was killed, and the walls to that room are all glass." My voice quivered as I dug my hand behind the couch cushions. "The videographer could have shot something in the background without even knowing."

"This is so exciting." Leatrice lifted the chair cushion and peered underneath. "What are we looking for?"

"The phone." I recovered it from under a blue fleece throw at the end of the couch. "I'm going to call the videographer and see if we can look at her footage. I just hope she isn't in a chatty mood today."

Leatrice hurried over and stood next to me while I dialed my favorite videographer's number by heart. Usually I loved gabbing with Joni about the latest industry gossip because she somehow knew the dirt on everyone, but today I didn't have time for chitchat. The phone rang a few times before a soft woman's voice answered. She sounded a little more like a phone sex operator than a videographer.

"This is Joni, how can I help—"

"Hey, it's Annabelle." I cut her off. "Sorry to be so

rushed, but do you have the footage from Saturday's wedding?"

Joni's voice switched from professional to relieved. "Hi, Annabelle. I'm glad it's you. I wanted to ask you what you think I should do with this video. I have great dressing and ceremony coverage, but after that it's all mostly mayhem. I do have a pretty good shot of everyone stampeding for the front door when the bride ran out into the courtyard in hysterics, but I don't think she's going to want that on her wedding video."

I cringed, remembering the chaos the bride had created once she came to and saw the dead chef and shattered ice sculpture. We hadn't been able to stop her from running into her cocktail party screaming bloody murder, and it hadn't helped matters that she had an enormous bruise on her cheek from where Fern had dropped her. No amount of editing could make that look pretty.

Joni continued, "I tried to do the last part in slow motion and put some romantic music in the background but it looks like a chase scene in a horror movie."

I groaned. "That bad?"

"Yep. It's going to take some major work to make this look halfway presentable. You don't think they're in a rush for this, do you?"

"No," I reassured her. "I don't think the video is their major concern right now." I doubted the bride would be eager to relive her wedding anytime soon since I'd heard that she'd gone to a holistic healing spa "for her nerves" in lieu of taking a honeymoon.

"I wish they'd gotten the short version instead of the long. I can make anything look great in a highlight reel. Maybe they'd agree to the short version, considering what happened."

"You haven't cut any footage yet, have you?" I held my breath for the answer.

"No way. I always keep the raw footage."

I let out a sigh of relief. Thank God she was as paranoid as me about keeping things.

"You never know what you might need later," Joni added. "I've had clients ask me to re-edit their video a year later because their grandmother died and they want more footage of her in the video. Or they want me to take out someone they aren't speaking to anymore. I even had one bride ask me to redo the entire video without the groom after they got divorced. Then there was the time that—"

"I need to ask you a huge favor, Joni." I knew this would be a hard sell. "I need to see the raw footage of the wedding."

She hesitated. "You know I don't like anyone to see the raw footage. It's like guests walking into the ballroom during setup. It ruins the magic of the finished product."

"You know I wouldn't ask if it wasn't important," I pleaded as Leatrice tugged on my sleeve.

"Tell her why we need it," Leatrice whispered.

"I only gave the raw footage to a bride once, and that was because it was a nudist wedding. I couldn't bear the thought of having to look at all those middle-aged naked people again."

"You shot a nudist wedding?" I forgot all about the murder for a moment. "Did you have to work in the nude?"

"Of course not," Joni gasped. "It was years ago, when I first started out in the business. I wouldn't take a nude wedding now."

I had no idea there was even a market for nudist weddings in D.C. I wondered what the proper wording on the invitation would be. Would Crane's even engrave the words "Clothing optional" in the bottom corner? Somehow I doubted it.

Leatrice poked me in the arm. "Well?"

"It's really important that I see the footage before it's edited," I begged. "I promise to return it to you as soon as I look at it."

"What are you looking for?"

If I really wanted her to show me the video, I'd need to tell her. "I think you might have recorded something through the glass walls of the Colonnade without knowing it."

"Really?" Joni sounded interested. "Like what?"

I exchanged a hopeful look with Leatrice. "Like the murder."

Chapter 16

"Did she agree to let you see it?" Kate's voice crackled through my cell phone as I walked down a side street toward Georgetown's business district. Georgetown already brimmed with energy at ten o'clock in the morning, with box trucks double-parked for their deliveries and boutique owners putting out sidewalk signs. I passed a New Age shop and noticed a sign advertising two-for-one chakra balancing, hanging amid the dangling crystals in the window. The sale would have tempted me if I had any idea what or where my chakras were.

"After I explained our theory about Georgia being framed, Joni was more than happy to help out." I glanced at my watch to make sure I still had enough time to get my morning frappuccino before meeting Kate. "She's bringing it by this afternoon."

"Our theory?" Kate sounded amused.

"Yes, our theory," I insisted, dashing across M Street before the light changed. "You, me, Richard, and Leatrice."

"Leatrice? How did she get involved in this?"

"You know Leatrice. Do you have to ask how she got herself involved?" I pushed the glass door to Starbucks open with my shoulder. The M Street coffee shop boasted lots of exposed brick, wood floors, and a large front window perfect for people watching. I sucked in the intoxicating aroma. Too bad I couldn't stand drinking the stuff unless it was mixed with enough chocolate and milk to make it nearly unrecognizable as coffee. With its whipped cream topping and faintest hint of coffee flavor, the frappuccino had been the heaven-sent answer to my coffee aversion, and now I'd become addicted to them. I ordered a Grande Light Mocha Frap and congratulated myself for not splurging on a Venti.

"This isn't turning into one of Leatrice's amateur sleuth projects, is it?" Kate asked. "Like the time she believed that she saw the old guy in 2B on *America's Most Wanted* and started following him around in a trench coat?"

"Of course not," I lied, knowing full well that Leatrice considered herself an equal partner in finding the real killer and clearing Georgia whether I liked it or not. I took my drink from the counter and walked back out to M Street. "Anyway, she hasn't followed that guy around in ages."

"That's because he moved, Annabelle. Not that I blame him. Who wants to be stalked by an eighty-year-old midget?"

I headed down a side street toward the harbor, taking small sips of my frappuccino. "She's not a midget, and you know it, Miss Smart Aleck."

"Maybe not legally, but she is pretty small," Kate argued good naturedly. "I think she's shrinking, too."

I arrived in front of the trendy flower shop, Lush. Monochromatic bunches of green and white flowers sat in galvanized buckets in the window. I tried the door. Locked. "How far away are you?"

"Right around the corner," she said as I saw her red car squeal around the curb, clipping the edge of the sidewalk. She parallel parked semilegally at the end of a row of cars and hopped out. "Are we the first ones here?"

"The boys must be running late," I called out as she strode across the street. By "the boys" I meant the two floral designers, Buster and Mack, who owned Lush and had become our new favorites. Their edgy modern designs were only one of the reasons they weren't your typical florists.

I heard a low rumble in the distance. In a few seconds two shiny chrome Harley-Davidson motorcycles appeared around the corner. They growled to a stop in front of us, and the massive riders, clad almost entirely in black leather, dismounted the bikes. The color of their goatees, one brown and one red, was the only way to tell them apart from a distance. They pulled off black helmets and pushed their riding goggles onto the tops of their heads. The "Mighty Morphin Flower Arrangers," as they preferred to be called in the biker world, had arrived.

"I swear those pants must be special order," Kate said under her breath. "I don't think Big and Tall shops in Washington carry leather. Not stretch leather, at least."

Buster of the dark brown goatee took two long steps to reach us. "Would you believe we got pulled over?"

"Apparently some bike gangs have been causing

trouble." Mack joined him, shaking his head. "This one had to tell the cop that we're florists on the way to a meeting with wedding planners."

"The officer wouldn't believe me." Buster took out a jumbled key ring and opened the door to the shop. "We had to wait while he ran our plates. And then he gave us tickets for speeding."

"Imagine," Kate muttered to me as we followed them inside.

They hung their helmets on hooks by the door and flipped on the track lighting that illuminated the window floral displays with colored light. A polished chrome rack held more galvanized buckets of blooms along the side wall, and a high metal worktable ran the length of the back, with several stools tucked underneath. The center of the room was empty. Minimalist, according to Buster and Mack. No stuffed animals, wicker baskets, or balloons in sight. Woe to the unsuspecting person who tried to order a "Pick Me Up" bouquet. The boys would slit their own wrists, then the customer's.

"Remind me why we're meeting with Nadine again." Mack tossed the bride's thick file on the table. "Correct me if I'm wrong, but isn't the wedding this Saturday?"

I hopped up onto a stool. "She's just getting nervous and wanted to take a final look at what you have in stock."

Buster waved a hand at the buckets of viburnum, hydrangea, and calla lilies. "Everything that's green or

124

white in here is hers. I hope she knows that it's too late to chicken out and go with some mamby-pamby blush tone scheme."

"Don't worry," I assured them. "She may be Southern, but she's not a girly-girl."

"She loves the look you boys put together," Kate added. "The lime green and white is going to look amazing in the Park Hyatt's modern ballroom."

Buster ran his finger down a desk calendar and glanced up. "You know where our other wedding is on Saturday, don't you?"

"The Fairmont," Mack chimed in. "People check in but they don't check out."

Buster ignored his counterpart, who giggled with Kate. "We don't know what's going on over there. I'm assuming the wedding is still on, but Georgia won't return any of our calls."

"You haven't heard, then?" I said. Darcy must not have made it to their messages yet. Surprising that the gossip hadn't reached them, though. Georgia had been one of the first big hotel catering execs to recommend the avant garde florists, and they adored her. "Georgia's been arrested for the murder of Chef Henri."

Both men gasped.

"When did this happen? We've been at a Christian biker rally and only got back last night," Buster said, his face stricken.

"She would never!" Mack's eyes were wide.

"Of course not," I agreed. "She's innocent."

Buster sank onto a stool, his face considerably paler. "Then why did they arrest her?"

"We think she's being set up by someone who wanted her out of the hotel," I said.

Mack blinked back tears. "Who would do such a thing?"

"We're not sure yet." I dug in my purse for a tissue and held it out to Mack. "The GM wanted to replace her, but the general consensus at the hotel is that he's too spineless to frame her for murder."

"Those other chefs at the Fairmont aren't too spineless." Mack blew his nose. "We've heard them talking when we're bringing flowers through the back of the hotel."

Buster nodded in agreement. "The sous chefs are almost as mean as Henri."

"Really?" Kate asked. "Maybe being scary is a chef thing."

"The real killer must have set up Georgia to throw the police off the trail," Buster said.

"Maybe. Kate and I have promised Georgia we'd nose around and see who hated Henri enough to kill him. If we can find the actual murderer, Georgia will be off the hook."

Buster's face relaxed. "If we hear anything interesting, we'll let you know."

"We should send flowers," Mack sniffled. "Do they let you get flowers in jail?"

Kate patted his hand. "I don't think so."

Mack dabbed at his eyes. "It's too horrible to think

126

about Georgia sitting in some drab cell with no decor."

"She'll be out before you know it," I tried to reassure them. "In the meantime, we still have a wedding on Saturday, remember?"

"Come on, you old softie." Buster gave Mack a hard pat on the back. "We won't let this get us down, will we? The bride is counting on us."

Mack bobbed his head up and down. "She's such a sweet little thing, too."

The glass door swung open and a cloud of cigarette smoke tumbled into the room. A waifishly thin woman followed, her brown hair tied up in a messy bun and a cell phone pressed to her ear.

"What do you mean they're bringing their kids?" she screamed into the phone, losing all remnants of her lilting Southern drawl. "This is an adult reception, Mother. That means no kids." A pause while she took a drag on her cigarette, then coughed. "He's your brother. You fix it." She snapped her phone shut and smiled at us. "Sorry about that. Last minute guest issues."

"Hi, Nadine," I sputtered as everyone else stared. "I didn't know you smoke."

"Oh, this?" She looked at the cigarette between her fingers. "I started this week to calm my nerves before the wedding. It doesn't seem to be working, though."

Leave it to a bride to try to reduce stress by picking up a habit that could kill you.

Mack grabbed a small glass bubble bowl from the shelf and rushed to hold it under her cigarette's long, dangling ash before it fell.

"Thanks." She took the bowl from Mack and pulled out a stool. "I'm still getting used to these things."

Buster regained his composure and opened her file. "Annabelle and Kate mentioned that you want to go over a few things for your wedding."

"I haven't been able to sleep because of my bouquet." Her slight Southern drawl had reappeared. I noticed that her eyes were bloodshot and rimmed in red. I could see that she was well on her way to a meltdown and wondered if she'd make it to Saturday. Or if we would.

Buster read the proposal. "We have down a hand-tied bouquet of white Casablanca lilies and white hydrangea."

"I'm sure it would be beautiful, but it doesn't seem to fit the modern theme we chose for the rest of the wedding." Nadine waved her cigarette, and Kate ducked as some ash flew her way.

Mack raised an eyebrow. "For the rest of the wedding we have chartreuse arrangements of pods and orchids with touches of lime green viburnum."

"Exactly." Nadine took a drag and blew out a stream of smoke. "I love that look. Can we do something like that for my bouquet, too?"

"Well . . ." Buster and Mack exchanged glances as Nadine slid off her stool and walked to the rows of tall metal flower buckets. She ran her hand along the blooms.

"This is it!" she cried out, pointing to a cluster of puffy green balls covered in soft fuzz. "I love these.

They're so untraditional. I want to carry a bouquet that no one has seen before."

"That would do the trick," Kate whispered to me.

"You want to carry a bouquet of only those?" Mack asked, the corner of his mouth twitching up.

Buster jumped in before Mack could say anything else. "Could we add some green orchids to fill it out?"

"That's fine. Just a few, though." Nadine threw her hand back, and her cigarette went flying. We all dodged as it landed in the corner and Buster stamped it out. The bride didn't even notice.

Nadine turned around and gave a long, satisfied sigh. "I feel much better now." She picked up her purse. "I've gotta run to my final dress fitting. I keep forgetting to eat, so they have to take it in again. Where did I put those cigarettes?"

"We should be all set, then," I said, hoping to put closure on her last minute changes. "We'll see you at the rehearsal."

Nadine opened the door and paused. "I'll call you this afternoon, Annabelle. I have a few changes to the passed hors d'oeuvres."

Before I could explain the problems involved with changing the menu three days before the wedding, she left.

"I'd say that went well," Kate said with a smirk.

"Oh, shut up." I pulled the bride's floral proposal out of my bag and turned to Buster and Mack. "So what's the name of the flower she changed her bouquet to?"

Buster grinned. "The bride chose a lovely bouquet of orchids and monkey balls," he said in a television announcer's voice.

I froze. "Excuse me?"

"You heard right." Mack beamed. He and Kate collapsed against each other in hysterical laughter.

I imagined the newspaper write-up in Nadine's South Carolina hometown. "The bride wore an ivory Vera Wang gown of silk organza embellished with seed pearls and carried a hand-tied bouquet of orchids and monkey balls."

Sometimes my job had its rewards.

Chapter 17

"I would have left it outside your door but your neighbor threatened to call the bomb squad on me," Joni said as Kate and I reached the landing to my apartment. She sat outside my apartment door wearing black pants and an untucked black T-shirt, with a paper shopping bag sitting in her lap. Leatrice hovered a few feet away in hot pink cowboy boots, giving her the evil eye.

"I noticed her following me in the building so I pretended to go in my apartment then I tailed her to your door." Leatrice didn't take her eyes off Joni. "I was about to make a citizen's arrest when you showed up."

Clearly, Leatrice had been watching too many episodes of *America's Most Wanted* again.

"I'm so sorry." I hurried to get my keys, giving Leatrice an evil eye of my own. "How long have you been waiting?"

"Not long." Joni got to her feet and held out the brown bag with handles. "I planned to leave the video hanging on the doorknob but apparently that's frowned upon in this building."

I looked at Leatrice over my shoulder. "This is Joni. The videographer I spoke to on the phone."

Leatrice began to fidget. "How did I know she was who she claimed to be? That bag could be a high-tech explosive, for all I know."

"Did you explain who you were?" I asked Joni.

"Several times." Joni arched an eyebrow. "I didn't know I needed to bring *two* forms of ID, though."

Kate gave her a nudge. "Well, you do look suspicious. Most terrorists are blond females, you know."

"She's wearing all black and carrying a package," Leatrice insisted. "You can't be too safe."

"This is Washington," Joni muttered. "Everyone wears black."

I pushed open my front door and ushered everyone inside, taking the bag from Joni. "Do you want to stay and watch it with us now that you're here?"

"Why not? It's one of the more interesting videos I've shot for pure entertainment value. There was that time that I shot the biker wedding and the bride wore white leather. I don't even know where you could find a leather wedding dress."

Thankfully, I didn't have any idea, either. The day a

bride asked me for a leather dress would be the day I hung up my wedding planner hat.

"And how could I forget the circus wedding?" Joni continued. "That couple was a bit off to begin with, though."

"Circus people are odd," I said.

"Oh, they weren't with the circus," Joni explained. "They just wanted a circus-themed wedding. The groom dressed like a ringmaster and the bride wore a tightrope walker's costume. All the guests had to dress up like clowns."

"That's one way to get a lower guest count," Kate muttered.

Leatrice brightened. "I wouldn't mind going to a wedding like that. I already have the outfit."

I shook my head. Why was I surprised?

"I'll put the tape in." Kate took the bag from me and headed toward my television stand tucked in the corner. "I'm dying to see what happened. We missed most of the action after the police detained us."

"After the bride ran into the courtyard screaming that her wedding vendors had murdered someone, it was pretty much pandemonium." Joni took a seat on the end of the couch and scooted over when Leatrice sat next to her. "I stopped shooting when the police came out. Luckily, I hadn't come anywhere near the crime scene, and they weren't interested in my ceremony footage."

"It didn't occur to the police that you might have inadvertently taped something through the glass walls?" I stood behind the couch and waited for Kate to finish putting the tape in the VCR.

"The officer who took our statements seemed really green," Joni said. "I don't think he'd been to many murder scenes."

Leatrice turned around to face me. "But you'll show this to the police if we find anything, right?"

"Of course. Once we've determined who the murderer is, I'll turn all the evidence over to the cops and let them make the arrest." I sighed. "We have to make sure our evidence outweighs the evidence they have against Georgia or it won't do any good."

"The tape's starting." Kate hunched in front of the TV. "Where's the remote to this thing?"

"I got it." I reached over to the wooden end table at the foot of the couch and grabbed the silver remote control. Kate stepped away from the television screen as it filled with an image of the bride getting her makeup done in the hotel suite. She wore jeans and a white button-down shirt, and her bridesmaids clustered around her nibbling on bagels and sipping champagne. She looked so happy that I cringed remembering her face when she saw the dead chef. I pushed the fast-forward button and the screen flashed through more dressing footage, shots of the outside of the church, and the world's fastest ceremony processional.

"Those are lovely dresses." Leatrice sniffled. "Do you think we could slow it down and watch some of the ceremony? Weddings are so beautiful, I always cry."

"No way." Kate shook her head. "It's a full Catholic mass. I sat through it once. No way am I sitting through it a second time."

We watched in fast forward as readers zipped up to the podium, the bride and groom exchanged vows in rapid fire, and the priest whizzed through communion. I leaned against the back of the couch wondering how long it would take us to get to the good part. You know you've done too many weddings when you consider a murder the most interesting part of a wedding video.

"Here comes the cocktail hour." Joni reached back and tugged on my sleeve.

I pressed Play and the courtyard came into view. Red lanterns hung from transparent wire and seemed to be suspended in midair. The camera panned the entire space then zoomed in on the bar set up against the Colonnade wall. As the camera slowly tightened its shot on the specialty drink menu in the red lacquered frame, I noticed a flicker of movement behind.

"Stop it there," Kate cried, pointing to the screen. "Someone's moving in the Colonnade."

"You're right." I paused the tape and forwarded it a frame at a time. The background was blurry, but I could make out two figures, both wearing white.

"Chefs' jackets." Kate slid close to the screen. "They must be wearing chefs' jackets."

I snapped my fingers. "Of course." We watched as the figures grappled in slow motion. Then one pushed the other behind the indoor gazebo. The next few seconds seemed to last forever as we waited to see what happened next. Finally one of the chefs emerged into the camera's view. Only one of the chefs. He left the room through the kitchen exit then came back in twice more, each time disappearing behind the gazebo. The killer certainly was thorough.

Kate turned around, her mouth hanging open. "Did we just see the murder?"

I nodded, unable to form a coherent sentence. I put the screen on freeze frame.

"It's not very easy to tell who it is, though." Leatrice squinted at the out of focus figures on the television.

"But we know two very important things now." My brain started working on overdrive as I focused on the screen. I walked to the TV and pointed to the figure who must have pushed Henri into the ice sculpture. "Whoever killed Henri wore a chef's jacket and had dark hair."

"You're right." Kate studied the screen intently. "That narrows it down some, but at the Fairmont there are lots of folks who work in the kitchen and have dark hair."

"Yes," I agreed. "But Georgia isn't one of them."

Chapter 18

"If the videotape clears Georgia of the murder, I don't understand why we don't take it to the police." Kate followed me through the Fairmont Hotel lobby, running to keep up.

After Joni had left and Leatrice went downstairs to get her magnifying glass so she could further inspect the video, Kate and I rushed down the back fire escape of my apartment building. Before Leatrice could notice we were gone, we'd hopped in my car and sped away. We knew she would have insisted on joining our search for dark-haired men in chef jackets, and it's hard to be inconspicuous with a little old lady in pink cowboy boots tagging along.

"For starters," I said, "the police are sure that Georgia is the killer, so it's going to take a lot of convincing for them to admit they made a mistake and let her go." I looked over my shoulder to make sure Kate kept up. "I also think we need to have more evidence about the actual murderer before we turn our information over. Which is why we're back at the Fairmont. To narrow down the list of dark-haired suspects."

"So you want us to build an entire case, and then hand it to the cops on a silver platter?"

I took the stairs to the second floor two at a time. "If that's the only way to be sure that Georgia is cleared of the murder, then yes."

"I don't know about this, Annabelle." Kate lowered her voice and closed the distance between us. "Do you think it's smart of us to poke around the hotel? What if the real killer doesn't want to be discovered?"

"We'll be discreet," I assured her. "I promised Georgia that I would ask around the hotel. I'm sure her colleagues will want to help her."

Kate shot me a sideways glance. "Except the one

that wanted her fired and the one who framed her for murder."

"Mr. Elliott isn't off my suspect list." I reached the second floor landing and paused to catch my breath. "The charming general manager may not have a lot of hair, but if I remember correctly, it is dark."

"So is Marcello's," Kate reminded me. "Are there no Scandinavian chefs in the city?"

"Believe me, if Richard hadn't been working with him at the Dumbarton House at the time of the murder, Marcello would be at the top of my list. But unless human cloning has come a lot further than I think, it would have been impossible for Marcello to kill Henri. I still think that Marcello might know something about who *did* kill his archenemy, though."

"Too bad he would never tell us." Kate followed me past the executive offices and through the door that led to the back hallways. "After the way he reacted when we mentioned Henri, I doubt he'd be willing to talk about the murder case again."

"Luckily we don't have to talk to him to get the information we need."

The halls in the back of the hotel were in stark contrast to the ones the guests saw. Painted cinder-block walls and utilitarian tile floors were a far cry from the hotel's trademark gleaming marble and polished glass. I stopped in front of the door to the employee cafeteria and motioned with a jerk of my head. "We have more than enough people right here who can lead us to the killer."

137

"Good thinking, Annie." Kate patted me on the shoulder. "If anyone is gossiping about the murder, this is the place we'll hear it."

I walked inside the employee cafeteria, which had recently been painted red. We were met by the buffet line, which reminded me of elementary school, with the rectangular metal pans of steaming food lined up behind glass hoods. We passed the hot food offerings and made our way down to the beverage station. The ice dispenser made a grinding noise but produced no ice, so we filled our tall paper cups with lukewarm Diet Coke. Nothing like a nice warm soda.

Once we had our drinks, I motioned for Kate to follow me into the sitting area filled with square tables and wooden chairs. A TV mounted on the wall played *Oprah*, and a cluster of women in housekeeping uniforms watched intently. A tall man I recognized as one of the security staff sat in a corner reading a newspaper. He glanced over his paper as we chose a table by the window that overlooked the roof of the Colonnade.

Kate slid her chair closer to me. "How are we going to get any information out of these people? No one is talking."

"I guess we wait until *Oprah* is over." I peeked at my watch. We had twenty minutes before the talk show queen released her siren's hold on the room.

"Do you ladies work in the hotel?" A deep voice startled me, and I jumped, spilling a bit of my soda on the table. No great loss. The security officer stood over me in his dark suit.

"Not exactly," I started to explain. "We're event planners, and we have an event in the hotel." Technically not for another two months, but not a complete lie, either.

He cleared his throat. "You can't be in the employee cafeteria if you're not an employee."

"Darcy O'Connell told us it would be okay for us to come here for a drink while we're working," Kate explained. Again, technically true. Darcy had said that during our last job at the Fairmont, but she probably hadn't intended for us to stop by randomly and hang out.

The officer narrowed his eyes at us and pulled out a walkie-talkie. "I'm going to have to confirm this with Miss O'Connell." He walked out of earshot and spoke low into the device.

"Don't worry, Annie." Kate took a sip of tepid soda and made a face. "Darcy will cover for us."

"So much for being low-key," I muttered. "The whole hotel knows we're here now."

"If we really wanted to blend in, we should have swiped a couple of housekeeping uniforms." Kate pointed a thumb toward the cluster of women in blue uniforms with white aprons.

I rolled my eyes. "This is not an episode of *I Love Lucy*. Do you really think the two of us would pass as maids, anyway? We're about twenty years younger than those women. And when is the last time you cleaned something?" Not that I was one to talk.

Kate made a face at me. "I can clean. I just choose not to most of the time."

"I'll bet you don't even own a toilet brush."

She gave me a horrified look. "Toilets use brushes?"

Before I could even begin to explain, my cell phone rang. I pulled it out of my purse and recognized the number on the caller ID.

"Hi, Nadine," I said as I flipped the phone open. "What's up?"

"I'm worried about my dress," she said in a shaky voice.

"What about it?" I kept my own voice calm. "Did something happen?"

"No, but the girls at the salon are concerned about the cathedral-length train getting crumpled when it's transported to my hotel suite. Can we get a stretch limo so the train doesn't have to be folded?"

I heard the unmistakable sound of smoke being exhaled. "You want me to get a limo for the dress?"

"Yes, the longest one they have. I'm going to pay one of the girls from the salon to ride with it."

God forbid the dress gets lonely on the ride across town.

I ignored Kate's muffled giggling. "No problem, Nadine."

"Oh, and one more thing," Nadine said. "Can you make sure the limo is black? Since my dress is technically ivory, I think a bright white limo would clash with it."

I paused to steady my voice and keep from laughing.

"You think a white limo will clash with the dress?"

Kate clamped her hand over her mouth and shook with silent laughter.

"Don't you?" The bride sounded shocked that I would question her.

"A black limo is no problem, Nadine. Call me if you think of anything else." I flipped the phone shut.

Kate wiped tears from her cheeks. "Ow. My sides hurt."

"It could be worse." I grinned. "At least she didn't insist on a police escort for the dress."

The security officer returned to our table, looking deflated. "Miss O'Connell gave you the okay to be here." He forced a smile before he turned away. "Have a nice day, ladies."

"We're lucky that Darcy is so cool," Kate said.

I bit the edge of my lip. "I'm sure she's wondering what we're up to."

"It's no big deal. She's on our side, remember? Didn't you see how stressed she was trying to keep up with Georgia's workload and her own? Darcy wants Georgia back more than anyone."

I looked past Kate and saw Darcy's face in the cafeteria doorway. She waved for us to come outside and then disappeared from view. I pulled Kate by the sleeve out of the cafeteria. Once in the hallway, I spotted Darcy behind a stack of plastic glass racks.

"What are you doing there?" I asked.

"Me?" she snapped, stepping from behind the racks. Her white blouse was half untucked from her black skirt and her hair looked like it hadn't been brushed in days. She'd gone from naughty librarian to demon-possessed librarian. "What are you doing here? Don't tell me you're actually here for a tasty snack in the employee cafeteria?"

"What happened to you?" Kate stared at Darcy.

"I pulled an all-nighter trying to catch up on work." Darcy rubbed her hands over her bloodshot eyes. "Sorry if I'm a little grumpy, but I'm exhausted. I can't take much more of this."

"Sorry if we took you away from something," I said. "We thought we might overhear something in the employee cafeteria that could help us prove Georgia's innocence."

"Really?" Darcy raised an eyebrow. "Did you have any luck?"

Kate shook her head. "We hoped to find some of the kitchen staff or chefs, but they aren't in there."

"The sous chefs are downstairs getting ready for a party in the ballroom," Darcy explained. "Most of the kitchen staff is probably there as well. Any reason why you want to talk to them?"

I looked at Kate, who nudged me to continue. "We found some evidence that shows that the actual killer had dark hair and wore a chef's jacket."

Darcy's mouth gaped open. "That's amazing. What kind of evidence?"

"The videographer shot part of the murder from the courtyard without even realizing it," Kate said. "We just watched the tape."

"Did you get a really clear look at the killer?" Darcy's eyes widened with excitement.

"It's fuzzy," I confessed. "We can't make out who did it, but we do know he had dark hair."

"If you're looking for dark-haired chefs, then you should talk to the two sous chefs and the pastry chef first," Darcy whispered. "All of them worked directly under Henri, all of them have dark hair, and all of them hated their boss. Emilio and Gunter should be working on the buffets in the ballroom foyer, and Jean may be setting up the dessert display already."

"Thanks, Darcy." I gave her arm a squeeze. "I know Georgia would be happy to know that she still has friends in the hotel."

Darcy nodded. "Georgia was a great boss, and I never knew how hard she worked until now. If I can do anything else to help, please let me know."

"Thanks," I said. "I guess we're going to go find some chefs."

Darcy took a few steps down the hall and called over her shoulder, "Don't let them intimidate you. They're like most chefs. Their bark is worse than their bite." She began to hum as she disappeared around a corner.

Kate gulped. "If one of these chefs killed Henri, I'm afraid we have more to be worried about than his bark."

Chapter 19

"This is a disgrace!" The distinctive disdain of the French accent carried from where Jean St. Jean stood examining a table of desserts on the other side of the ballroom. *"Mon dieu!* Who put the tartlets on a mirrored tile?"

Kate took a baby step back out into the hallway before I caught her by the arm and pulled her into the room. The large ballroom was filled with rows of tables draped in white cotton cloths, and matching napkins stood in fan folds on the white base plates. Each table had the same low glass bowl of red and gold flowers. This party definitely had the feel of a corporate event.

I dragged Kate behind me as I weaved my way through the maze of tables to where Jean stood muttering to himself at the dessert display. He wore a pristine white jacket over dark billowy pants and a tall chef's hat perched on his brown wavy hair.

He jumped when he heard us behind him. "Who are you?"

"Just party planners," I responded, hoping he would assume that I meant we were the party planners for this event. Not a lie, I reasoned to myself. An omission.

"Of course." He gave a curt nod of his head. "I am Jean St. Jean, the pastry chef for the Fairmont Hotel. I was merely inspecting the work of my subordinates before the party begins."

"We've heard wonderful things about your work." I nudged Kate. "Haven't we?"

"Absolutely." Kate bobbed her head eagerly. "The Fairmont is known for having some of the best chefs in the city."

Jean St. Jean gave a smug smile. "It is nice to be recognized for one's excellence." Boy, this guy was full of himself.

"Such a shame that you lost the real culinary genius in the hotel, though." I shook my head and didn't take my eyes off St. Jean.

His smile disappeared and his eyes flashed with anger. "They're saying that Henri was the genius? Idiots."

"Well, he was the head chef, wasn't he?" Kate asked in an innocent voice.

"Not because of culinary skill, I assure you," the pastry chef fumed. "The man didn't have as much talent in his entire body as I do in my little finger. The only ideas he ever had were ones he stole from others."

"Did he steal your ideas?" I pressed.

"He stole from everyone. If any one of his chefs had an idea, Henri claimed it as his own and took the glory." St. Jean slammed his hand down on the dessert display, and the rows of tiny truffles began to roll around.

This guy had some impulse control issues.

"So he wasn't very popular among the other chefs?" I caught a truffle as it headed for the edge of the table.

St. Jean laughed derisively. "We don't miss him, if that's what you mean to ask."

"Were you here the day of the murder?" I said, knowing full well that he had been.

"Of course." He turned his attention back to the dessert table. "I created the wedding cake. Such a pity the guests never saw it. It was quite a masterpiece."

I vaguely remembered the four-tiered stacked cake ornamented with the red Chinese symbol for double happiness on each layer. I knew it had been set up on the baby grand piano in the alcove, but I couldn't recall if I had seen it before or after I found the body.

"So you were in the Colonnade around the time of the murder?" I watched as he realigned the truffles.

The chef stopped what he was doing and looked up at me. "I set up the cake during the cocktail hour, but Henri was nowhere to be seen when I left the room."

"Are you sure?" Kate folded her arms over her chest.

"I think I would have noticed him." His face flushed. "Why so many questions?"

"Just curious," I said. "Did you see anyone else in the room when you were there?"

"Gunter and Emilio came in to check the stations as I left. We were all in and out of the room setting up the wedding. Nothing unusual about that." He narrowed his eyes. "Who did you say you were again?"

"Nobody important." I backed away. "We'll let you get back to your work."

"You might want to rethink the mirror tiles, though,"

Kate added as she followed me. Jean St. Jean scowled and stalked off through the back kitchen doors of the ballroom.

"Well, that was interesting," I said. "He wasn't shy about hating Henri."

"Did you believe his alibi?"

I shrugged. "I wouldn't put the murder past him, but let's see if anyone corroborates his story."

"So one down, two to go." Kate navigated through the sea of tables toward the doors.

I pressed my lips together. "We'd better find Gunter and Emilio before our French friend warns them. He seemed suspicious of our questions."

"Maybe you should let me lead the next interrogation. I have more experience charming things out of men."

Kate had a point. "Be my guest." I held open the doors to the foyer. Two chefs in matching white jackets stood with their backs to us. Jackpot.

"Why must you insist on making the crudités display so Prussian?" one of the chefs said to the other, rolling his r's and laughing.

"You have no appreciation for the precision of cooking," the other replied in a heavy accent that I placed somewhere between Germany and Eastern Europe. I could only assume this was Gunter. His dark hair was cropped close to his head, and his jacket looked like it had been starched until it could stand on its own.

"And you have no appreciation for its passion."

147

I'd heard of Emilio's reputation for avidly pursuing passions in and out of the kitchen.

Kate cleared her throat, and both men looked over their shoulders at us. Emilio did a double take, and grinned at Kate like a wolf about to pounce.

"Perhaps these lovely women would give us their opinion." The Latin chef's brown hair fell in curls around his face.

Gunter returned to his straight rows of vegetables with a measuring tape. "I must finish my work without delay."

"We were admiring your artistry." Kate approached a table set with various clay bowls of Spanish tapas and ran a finger languidly around one of the bowls. "I love a man who's passionate about his work."

Emilio raised his eyebrows. "It takes a good eye to recognize culinary beauty. You must appreciate the art of food."

"I appreciate a lot of things," Kate purred. Man, she was pouring it on thick. I wondered if I should remind her to question them, not seduce them.

"Are you staying in the hotel?" Emilio leaned close to Kate. "Perhaps we could meet for drinks after I get off."

"We're actually working, too." Kate explained. "We're party planners."

"So you work here often?" He ran his tongue along his bottom lip.

Kate nodded. "We'll be here more now that Chef Henri is gone."

"Don't tell me he terrorized you." Emilio took Kate's hand with a concerned look on his face. "That man had no shame."

"He got what he deserved," Gunter said over his shoulder.

"Were you here when he was murdered?" Kate asked Emilio in a conspiratorial whisper. "Did you see the body?"

"Of course we were here." Emilio puffed out his chest.

Gunter turned around with a snap. "We checked the stations, and then left the room together before Chef Henri was murdered. Just like we told the police."

"That's right." Emilio bobbed his head in agreement. "We never saw the body."

Kate rubbed her hands together. "How exciting to have been in the room only moments before a murder took place. Did you see anything suspicious? Maybe someone else went into the room after you?"

"The banquet captain, Reg, and the general manager were coming in the main entrance of the Colonnade as we left through the kitchen doors." Emilio darted a glance at Gunter. "We didn't go back to the Colonnade, though, so we never saw when they left."

Kate pressed a hand on Emilio's arm. "I'll bet the police were really interested in your story."

"We were in the kitchens working at the time of the murder, so we couldn't tell them much." Emilio shrugged.

"Was Jean with you, as well?" I tapped my foot on the carpet.

"We were all together." Gunter's face wore no expression. "Excuse me. I must return to the kitchen."

Kate watched the stiff chef walk away. "I hope we didn't upset him by talking about the murder. It's so fascinating that it happened right here in this very hotel."

Emilio dismissed Gunter's behavior with a wave of his hand. "He's not much of a talker. His closest friend is that measuring tape." He glanced at his watch, and his eyes widened. "You must forgive me, ladies. I also must get back to work."

"Of course," Kate said. "Nice meeting you."

Emilio gave a parting leer. "I hope we meet again soon. Perhaps you can give me your number?"

"Sure." Kate turned to me. "Do you have a pen?"

I dug in my bag for a pen and handed it to her.

Kate scrawled something on a page in her purse-size day planner and ripped it out. She folded it in half and tucked it into the pocket of the chef's jacket.

He patted the note and then gave Kate a seductive smile and me a cursory glance before darting through the banquet doors.

Kate sighed. "Sorry that wasn't more helpful. At least we found out that the banquet captain and the GM were in the room around the time of the murder, too."

"Are you kidding? We found out a lot more than that. I think he's hiding something."

"Me, too," Kate said eagerly, and then a puzzled expression crossed her face. "Wait. Which one?"

I rolled my eyes. "Gunter, of course."

"Why?" Kate asked. "He said almost nothing."

"Exactly. His answers were too easy. Almost like he rehearsed them. I think he knows more about the murder than he's letting on."

"Emilio seemed nice enough."

"Are you sure it was a good idea to give him your number, though?" I asked as Kate handed me back my pen.

"Oh, don't worry. I didn't give him my number." She shook her head seriously. "I gave him yours."

Chapter 20

"You did what?" I stared at Kate in shock.

"Emilio might have gotten suspicious if I refused to give him my number."

"But why give him mine?"

Kate shrugged. "You told me I shouldn't play the field so much."

"But I should?" Before I could launch into a proper tirade, my cell phone rang and I flipped it open. "Wedding Belles, this is Annabelle."

"Annabelle, honey. This is Darla Douglas." The voice slurred slightly. "Debbie and I have a quickie question for you."

I looked at my watch. It was already afternoon, so

they must be past their first cocktail of the day.

"We're thinking of doing the groom's cake in the shape of Turner's black lab, Binger. Do you know a cake baker who could do that for us?" She paused and took a drink of something. "He just adored that dog."

Past tense? I gulped. "Binger isn't alive?"

"No, but we think it would be a special way to remember him on the wedding day."

By serving him to the guests? I rubbed my head. "Okay, can you send me a picture of the dog?"

"We'll pop one right in the mail to you. Now, does this baker do a good rum cake?"

I cringed at the thought of the booze-themed wedding that seemed to be solidifying. "Of course, but you can do a tasting to make sure."

"That's a great idea. We want to make sure it's as flavorful as my grandmother's recipe. Most people go too light on the rum."

Nothing like getting drunk off a slice of the beloved, deceased Binger.

"I'll set up the tasting for you," I said. "How's next week?"

"Perfect. I'd better run. Debbie and I don't want to miss our court time at the club."

I hung up my phone. "Remind me not to eat the groom's cake at the Douglas wedding."

"Let me guess, martini flavored?" Kate asked.

"Close enough," I groaned. "Rum cake in the shape of a dead dog."

"It must be a wedding." A deep voice from behind startled me.

I spun around, clutching my hand to my heart. "Reg! Don't sneak up on people like that." My heart raced as I wondered how much he'd heard.

The tall, wiry banquet captain laughed as Kate clutched my arm. "D-Didn't mean to scare you."

"Thanks," Kate mumbled as she walked to a nearby cocktail table and sat down. "I think I lost a year off my life."

"What are you two doing back here so soon?" Reg ran a hand through his unruly brown hair. "I thought you'd steer clear of this place after the police finally let you go."

Kate nodded. "That would make sense, but we're trying to help—"

"Darcy." I jumped in before Kate could mention Georgia and tip off one of our suspects. "We stopped by to see if we could help Darcy since she's so swamped with work now that Georgia is gone."

Reg's face clouded. "Poor Georgia. She didn't have anything to do with Henri's murder."

"How can you be sure?" I took a seat next to Kate. This didn't sound like someone who wanted to frame her for murder.

"Georgia is too s-s-sweet to hurt anyone," he insisted, with a slight stutter. "You can tell about people, and Georgia is no killer."

"Then who do you think killed Henri?" Kate laced her fingers together and rested her chin on them.

Reg pressed his lips together and sank into a chair across from us. "I don't know. If I had any clue that could help Georgia, I would've told the police already."

"Georgia is lucky to have a friend like you, Reg," I said.

"I don't think she considers me a friend." Reg smiled weakly. "We didn't run in the same circles. She's much too glamorous to socialize with a banquet captain."

I looked at the shy banquet captain with cowlicks pushing his hair in all directions and a stutter that emerged when he was nervous. Did Reg have a crush on Georgia?

"I t-t-tried to visit her in jail, but they wouldn't let me in," he continued, his face flushed pink. "I wanted her to know that some people still care about her."

"Listen, Reg." I grabbed his hand. "Did you see anyone go into the Colonnade before Henri was murdered?"

"I went in to double-check the room setup, but Henri wasn't there. The waiters were at the cocktail hour since we'd set up the room so early, so it was only me."

"Did you see any of the chefs in the room?" Kate asked.

He chewed on his lower lip as he thought. "Gunter and Emilio were leaving through the back kitchen door as I came in."

So they were telling the truth. "What about Jean?"

154

"Nope." He shook his head. "The cake was already set up, and I didn't see him all afternoon."

"And Mr. Elliott?" I asked. Emilio had claimed that Reg had been with the general manager.

Reg frowned. "The GM followed me in the room. He was on the warpath that day."

"What do you mean?" Kate raised an eyebrow.

"Some days he seemed to look for something or someone to p-p-pick on. Saturday was one of those days."

"Did he find anything?" I pressed.

"I don't know," Reg said. "He told me to leave the Colonnade so that the photographer could get some room shots before the guests came in. The next thing I knew, Henri was dead, and the police were swarming the place."

"Mr. Elliott was setting up room shots?" I exchanged a look with Kate. We both knew the photographer hadn't been in the hotel until after the murder took place.

Reg nodded. "If a wedding made the hotel look good, he always got promotional pictures."

The wheels in my head were slow to turn. What would Mr. Elliott gain by killing Henri? "Reg, is there any reason Mr. Elliott would've wanted Henri dead? Anything at all?"

"No one really liked Henri," Reg explained. Hardly breaking news. "But he was the highest-paid employee, aside from the general manager himself. Henri caused lots of problems in the hotel, but he

155

would have created even more if they tried to fire him."

"Did Mr. Elliot want to fire Henri?" I cast a glance over my shoulder as a bartender brought a rack of glasses to the bar at the end of the foyer. "We heard he'd been looking for a reason to fire Georgia."

"I think he would have been happy to get a trouble-maker like Henri out of the hotel," Reg whispered. "He seemed intimidated by Georgia, so maybe he tried to kill two birds with one stone."

My mouth fell open. "You think this was the GM's idea of budget cuts?"

"Well, it does save on a severance package," Kate said.

"As horrible as Mr. Elliott sounds," I said, "I have a hard time believing that he killed Henri just so he wouldn't have to fire him."

Reg grimaced. "You don't know the people in Human Resources, do you?"

"Annie, this would explain why one person would kill Henri and frame Georgia for it," Kate said. "It sounds like Mr. Elliott was the last person in the Colonnade before Henri's death."

I nodded as I processed our clues. Mr. Elliott could have easily gotten a chef's jacket from the kitchen and confronted Henri once he had assured himself that no one would disturb the "room shots." It would've taken only a few minutes to push Henri into the ice sculpture, then ditch the jacket and return to the front of the hotel.

I had one last question for Reg. "Do you think there's any reason why Gunter would have acted strange when we questioned him?"

"Are you sure that Gunter wasn't being himself? He's never been the friendliest fellow." Reg gave an almost apologetic laugh.

"That's putting it mildly," Kate said.

"He's not very social with the staff," Reg continued. "He seems to tolerate his fellow chefs, but that's about it. Never really fit in. And he drives them all crazy with his tape measure. I doubt he'll stay at the hotel once he gets his green card and can change jobs."

"Thanks, Reg." I stood up as I saw a few people begin to wander down the stairs. "You've been a lot of help."

Reg reached out and shook my hand tentatively. "Will you tell Georgia that we all miss her?"

"Of course, Reg." I squeezed his hand. "I'll tell her that you asked about her."

Reg flushed and stepped away. "Tell her I'd do anything to help her."

"Come on." I pulled Kate by the sleeve toward the elevators. "I think we've gotten all the information we're going to get today."

"Don't you want to talk to Gunter again?" Kate asked. "I thought you said he was hiding something."

"I did." I pressed the elevator call button in rapid fire. "I still think he knows more than he said. Maybe he's even covering for Mr. Elliott. But I don't think we're going to convince him to spill his guts."

157

"What about Mr. Elliott?" Kate followed me into the empty elevator car. "He seems guiltier every second."

"And more dangerous," I agreed as the elevator surged up toward the lobby. We were quiet for several seconds, then I said, "If he planned Henri's murder to get rid of two problem employees, then he won't be very willing to talk to anyone about it."

"So what do we do next?" Kate hurried behind me as I exited the elevator.

"I think it's time to give some of our information to the police." I dug in my purse for my valet parking ticket. "They can question Gunter and Mr. Elliott and get more information than we can."

"I thought you didn't trust the police to keep looking for the killer since they have Georgia in custody."

I pushed through the glass revolving doors that led out of the hotel. "I don't, but we have so much information now that they can't ignore it." I handed my parking ticket to the valet attendant and held up a finger. "First, we have the video, which shows that the murderer was a dark-haired man in a chef's jacket. Second, we've determined that all the chefs came in and out of the Colonnade prior to the murder. Unfortunately, they all corroborate each other's alibis. Emilio and Gunter saw Mr. Elliott and Reg come into the room after they left, and I'll bet Gunter saw more than that by the way he clammed up. We have a general manager who everyone knew wanted Georgia fired and apparently also wanted Henri out. He cleared the room for photos that you and I know couldn't have taken place because there was no photographer. That gives him motive and opportunity." I sucked in a breath. "And he has dark hair. Well, some at least."

"You think Gunter is covering for him?"

I nodded. "It seems like all the chefs are concerned with saving their own necks. Turning in the boss isn't the smartest move, especially if your green card is dependent on keeping your job. I wouldn't be surprised if all the chefs know more than they're willing to admit."

Kate gave a low whistle. "What a hornet's vest!"

Chapter 21

"Help has arrived," Richard called out as he swung his silver convertible Mercedes into the Fairmont's circular drive with a squeal of tires.

Kate hopped into the backseat and I slid into the front, giving Richard a sheepish smile. "Thanks for coming. I don't know what they did with my car."

"We waited for over an hour, and they still couldn't find it." Kate stuck her head between the two front seats. "At least they didn't make us pay."

"This is a bad sign, darlings." Richard pulled the car back onto Twenty-fourth Street and slid a pair of sunglasses on. "First your car is stolen, next we're all going to find ourselves bound and gagged and being shipped off to Abu Dhabi. You know I would be a prime target for white slavery."

"I would only assume." I rolled my eyes. What a drama queen. "This is nothing more than bad luck."

"Don't you think it's an awfully big coincidence that when you start your own mini murder investigation, your car disappears?" Richard peered at me over his dark glasses. "And that the suspects you're questioning happen to have access to the garage where your car is parked?"

"I think the chances are greater that the valet lost the ticket than that someone intentionally took my car," I argued.

"Don't forget the time a parking attendant crashed my car driving it up the garage ramp." Kate raised her voice above the traffic. "Parking attendants aren't the sharpest knives in the door."

"It's drawer." I shot a look over my shoulder. "And thanks, that's very comforting. I'm sure they'll find my car."

"You're out of your mind if you think this is some wild coincidence," Richard insisted. "I told you not to stick your nose in this case."

I gaped at Richard. "No, you didn't."

"I didn't?" He looked genuinely surprised. "Well, I certainly meant to. Consider this a slightly belated warning not to meddle anymore."

"I'll consider myself warned." I settled back in my seat and looked around M Street as we entered Georgetown. Narrow restaurants with brightly colored awnings lined the streets, and a row of black sedans and a couple of motorcycle cops sat in front of the Four Seasons Hotel across the street. I wondered which dignitary was in town this time.

"I know that look," Richard sighed. "You have absolutely no intention of minding your own business, do you? Why would this day be any different? Why doesn't anyone listen to me?"

Soap operas had less angst than this. "I'll make a deal with you, Richard. If you give us a ride to the police station, I'll turn over my evidence to Detective Reese and retire from the case."

"Really?" Richard gave me a suspicious look. "What's the catch?"

"No catch." I shrugged. "Let me run inside my apartment and grab the videotape, and then we can go straight to the police."

"What videotape?" Richard made a sharp right on Thirtieth Street and sped around a car trying to parallel park.

"The video that shows the murder of Chef Henri," Kate chimed in from the backseat. "The wedding videographer didn't even know she'd filmed it through the glass walls."

Richard's eyes widened as he paused momentarily at a stop sign. "Can you tell who the killer is?"

"It's not totally clear," I confessed. "But you can see that whoever did it has dark hair and is wearing a white chef's jacket."

Richard drummed his fingers on the steering wheel. "So another chef did kill him."

"Or someone who snagged a chef's jacket." Kate waved a finger in the air. "It would have been a great disguise."

Richard pulled to a stop in front of my building. "So, did you narrow down the field of dark-haired people at the hotel?"

"I thought you were against snooping around. I wouldn't dream of sullying you with our ill-gotten information." I opened my door and blew him a kiss while Kate stifled her laughter. "I'll be back in a flash."

I pushed open the heavy front doors of my narrow stone building and ran up the stairs two at a time. I caught my breath when I reached my apartment on the third floor and took a second to listen for footsteps or squeaking clothing. So far no sign of Leatrice. I dashed into my apartment, grabbed the videotape off the top of the VCR, and shoved it back in the paper bag it had arrived in. I went back down the stairs at a more leisurely pace since apparently I didn't need to dodge Leatrice this time. I walked out of my building and stopped short. I'd spoken too soon.

Leatrice sat in the backseat next to Kate, wearing a hot pink cowgirl hat accented with white rickrack. Richard's lips were pressed together so tightly they'd disappeared entirely.

"Leatrice." I tried to sound happy to see her. "What are you doing?"

"Kate told me that we're taking the video to the police station." Leatrice beamed. "You don't think I'd miss that, do you?"

162

I arched an eyebrow at Kate. Richard looked as if he couldn't decide which one to throttle first.

Kate batted her eyelashes. "I may have mentioned something."

The chances of convincing Leatrice to stay behind were slim to none, and I didn't relish the idea of dragging a little old lady kicking and screaming out of a car in broad daylight. Richard looked like he was pondering the same options.

"No jury in the world would convict us," Richard finally said in a conspiratorial whisper. "Not when we admit the hat as evidence."

I ignored him and got in the car. "Okay, Leatrice, you can come, but we're only going to be a few minutes. We're dropping the tape off and leaving. I'm afraid it's not going to be very exciting."

"Don't you worry, dearie. It beats watching reruns on the Game Show channel."

Richard adjusted his rearview mirror in a huff. "The hat has got to go. I can't see a thing behind me."

"But it matches the boots." Leatrice raised a hot pink cowboy boot in the air for inspection. They did, indeed, appear to be a matching set. "They'll look silly without the hat."

"I don't think the hat deserves all the blame," Richard muttered.

"How about you take it off for the ride over?" I bargained. "So it won't blow away?"

"Good thinking." Leatrice took off the hat and gave me a pat on the shoulder.

Richard glanced over at me before he gunned the engine. I'd be paying for this for the next decade.

Despite Leatrice's insistence on singing "One Hundred Bottles of Beer on the Wall" during the drive and Richard's noticeable acceleration as each bottle of beer happened to fall, we arrived in front of the police station in one piece.

"No singing," I said as we walked up the sidewalk to the glass front doors. "We're here to turn this over to Reese, explain what we've learned, and leave."

Leatrice nodded silently as she bounced through the door on the toes of her boots. The officer at the desk glanced up, and then did a double take when he saw Leatrice. I guess it wasn't every day you saw an elderly woman in pink cowgirl regalia. Especially in D.C.

"Wait here," I said to Leatrice.

She and Kate sat on two plastic chairs lined against the wood-paneled wall while Richard followed me to the desk. Clearly he'd rather take his chances with the cops than be associated with Leatrice.

"I'm here to see Detective Reese. Is he in?" I asked the desk clerk. "I need to drop something off."

"Oh, yeah?" The tall, pasty officer looked past me to where Leatrice sat swinging her legs. "What's her name?"

"No, I'm not dropping off a person," I explained.

Richard elbowed me. "This is a once-in-a-lifetime chance. Don't be a fool. Take it."

I shot him a look and then turned back to the cop.

"I'm dropping off evidence in a murder case." I held up the paper bag by its handles.

The officer's eyes widened and he stroked his thin blond mustache. "He's questioning someone, but I'll see if he can be disturbed."

"It's not too late to change your mind," Richard whispered as the cop disappeared in the back. "I'm sure they'd take good care of her."

"Very funny, Richard. You know Leatrice isn't crazy. She's just a bit colorful." I followed Richard's gaze and saw that Leatrice had twisted her boots around so that her feet looked like they pointed in the wrong direction. She and Kate were giggling like fiends.

Richard put his hands on his hips. "I say we leave them both."

"What's this about evidence?" Detective Reese's gruff voice startled me and I spun around. He wore a rumpled shirt and at least a day's growth of stubble. "We're kind of swamped with homicides right now."

My cheeks got warm when I saw him, but immediately cooled when I remembered his bleached blonde cupcake at the restaurant. I cleared my throat. "We didn't mean to disturb you, but we have something that might change your mind about Georgia."

"I doubt it." He ran a hand through his hair. "I'm finishing an interview with another hotel witness, and it's not looking good for your friend."

I held out the bag. "Wait until you watch this. The wedding videographer inadvertently caught the murder on tape through the glass walls while she filmed in the courtyard."

Reese took the bag from me and pulled out the video. "You've watched it?"

I nodded. "It's not crystal clear, but you can tell that the person who killed Henri had dark hair and wore a chef's jacket."

Reese raised an eyebrow and tapped his fingers on the black cassette. "This might be interesting."

"And we talked to the chefs in the hotel today," I said, pausing to take a quick breath. "They all have alibis, but the sous chef, Gunter, seemed to be hiding something. We think he may be covering for someone. The general manager cleared out the Colonnade for a photographer to take room shots, but the photographer wasn't even in the hotel at the time. Maybe Gunter saw the GM with Henri but is afraid to say anything because he might lose his job and his chance for a green card."

"So much for letting us do our job." Reese leveled his eyes at me. "If you're doing so well on your own, why give this to me?"

"For God's sake, don't encourage her," Richard groaned.

"We don't think that we can get any more information out of the suspects. We figured we'd turn over our evidence and you could interrogate Gunter and the general manager and let Georgia go."

"I'm afraid it won't be that simple." Reese dropped the cassette back in the bag. "Gunter won't implicate the GM."

166

I balled my hands into fists. "How do you know unless you try?"

"I know because he's dead. We got a call only a couple of minutes ago that one of the Fairmont chefs accidentally electrocuted himself. I was about to head out to join the investigation when you arrived."

"You're sure it's Gunter?" I felt light-headed.

"Yep. It's a hard name to forget." Reese patted me on the shoulder. "Bad luck for him and you, huh?"

I felt numb. Gunter's death didn't have anything to do with bad luck. I felt more convinced than ever that he'd known something about Henri's death. And unfortunately the murderer had made sure he'd never get the chance to tell anyone.

Chapter 22

"You don't look so good, dearie." Leatrice watched me collapse onto my couch. "Maybe you need something cool to drink."

"I'll check out the refrigerator," Richard called over his shoulder as he walked from my living room to the kitchen. He pulled open the wooden shutters that created a window between the two rooms. "Make sure she doesn't faint."

"I'm fine," I lied. Richard had threatened to throw Leatrice's hat into traffic if she sang again, so the ride home from the police station had been mercifully quiet, but my head still throbbed. It was hard to believe that we'd spoken to Gunter only a couple of hours ago and now he was dead. I couldn't help thinking that my meddling was the reason.

"You didn't get this upset when you saw Henri's body." Kate tossed her shoes off and perched on the arm of the couch. "What gives?"

"What if we're the reason he's dead?" I asked, my throat dry. "Obviously he was killed so he couldn't talk, and we're the ones trying to get people to talk."

"You can't blame yourself for this." Kate shook her head. "Maybe it was an accident."

"Too coincidental," I said firmly. "I'm starting to think Richard is right about my car, too. Maybe the real killer is sending us some warnings to back off."

"Did I hear you say that I'm right? Will wonders never cease?" Richard bounced out of the kitchen carrying a glass of something brown. He handed it to me. "It's slightly flat Coke, but in this case it'll be good for you."

I took a drink. Sad to say, I was getting used to flat soda. "Poor Gunter. Now we'll never know what he was hiding."

"But we can be pretty sure he saw something that someone didn't want him to share with you or the police," Leatrice said. "You must have struck a nerve with your questioning."

"That's right, Annabelle," Kate agreed. "We must have been on the right track or the real killer wouldn't have felt threatened enough to murder again."

"Is that supposed to be comforting?" Richard shuddered. "You girls are lucky you got out of there alive."

"I don't think *we're* in danger," I said, dismissing Richard's concern.

"Oh really?" Richard began pacing in front of my windows. "A smart killer would go straight to the source. Why not get rid of the two people who are poking around and stirring up trouble? The police aren't looking for more suspects, so the murderer is home free as long as you two don't mess everything up."

I opened my mouth to argue and then stopped. He had a point. Maybe our harmless investigation wasn't so harmless after all. "But who's the most likely killer out of the people who knew we were asking questions about Henri's death?"

"I don't think we can assume that only the people we talked to knew we were there," Kate said. "Word travels fast."

"Why don't we write down all the suspects?" Leatrice began searching for some blank paper on my coffee table. She produced a legal pad from under a pile of magazines and pulled a miniature pencil from her pocket.

Richard let out a long breath. "This seems rather pointless since you're officially retired from your investigation, right?"

"It can't hurt to talk about the case." I shifted in my seat and avoided his eyes.

"There's Mr. Elliott, the hotel's general manager," Kate began. "Nobody likes him, and he wanted to get rid of both Georgia and Henri. He got everyone out of the room where the murder took place under false pretense, too."

Leatrice scratched feverishly in the pad. "That's good. Motive and opportunity. Who's next?"

"I guess the remaining chefs we spoke to. Jean and Emilio. Neither of them were too fond of their boss, and both were in the room prior to the murder. But they have alibis." I downed the last of the flat soda and put the glass on the floor. "Jean is a bit of a prima donna, and Emilio is the in-house Casanova."

"Is he still chasing skirts?" Richard smirked. "He worked for me a few years back. I was always afraid I'd open a kitchen door and find him romancing a prep cook on the counter."

Leatrice's eyebrows popped up. "That doesn't sound very sanitary."

"I doubt Emilio's love life has anything to do with the murder." I tried to change the subject before Leatrice asked for more details. "I would normally list the banquet captain, Reg, as a suspect but I think he's too in love with Georgia to frame her for murder."

"He could have committed the crime without meaning for Georgia to get arrested for it," Kate suggested.

"Good point." I nodded. "That would explain why he's so distraught over her arrest. Maybe he killed Henri to help Georgia, then his plan backfired."

"But do you really think Reg could have murdered someone?" Kate asked me. "He can barely get two sentences out without tripping over his words."

"I know, but if we eliminate everyone we think is too nice to be a killer, our list will only have one name—Mr. Elliott. And Darcy and Hugh swear that he's too spineless to do it."

"Who are Darcy and Hugh?" Leatrice started to write their names down.

"Darcy has been Georgia's assistant for the past three years and Hugh is the head concierge," Kate explained.

"Talk about people who are too mild mannered to kill someone, unless Hugh could get first row Kennedy Center tickets out of it." I grinned. "Neither of them have motives, either."

Leatrice frowned and tapped the notepad with her pencil. "I'll leave them on the list, anyway. Do you have any suspects who don't work in the hotel? It sounds like your victim might have had enemies all over town."

I avoided Richard's gaze. "There is another chef who hated Henri enough to kill him."

"There is no way Marcello could have had anything to do with Henri's death," Richard insisted. "I was with him setting up for a wedding at Dumbarton House at the precise time Henri was murdered."

Leatrice shook her head. "That doesn't make him a very good suspect, then."

"No, it does put a wrinkle in things," I admitted.

Leatrice looked at her notes and then looked up at us. "Someone isn't what they seem to be."

I snapped my fingers. "She's right. What do we really know about these people? We need to research our suspects. Find out about their pasts. Where else they worked in town, their reputations, their personal lives. Maybe that will give us the clues we need to piece it all together."

Richard glared at me. "Might I remind you that you swore off meddling only an hour ago?"

"Annabelle doesn't have to do it." Kate hopped up. "I've got lots of contacts in hotels."

"Do you mean contacts or ex-boyfriends?" Richard batted his eyelashes at her.

Kate stuck her tongue out at him. "Jealous?"

"Hardly." Richard snatched my empty glass from the floor and flounced off to the kitchen.

"Listen." Kate lowered her voice. "I have to run a few errands tomorrow, so why don't I pop by some of the hotels and see what I can dig up?"

"Alone?" I asked. "After what happened today, are you sure that's safe?"

"I could go with you," Leatrice offered.

"No," Kate said forcefully, and then relaxed into a smile. "I'll be fine. None of the other hotels have murderers on the loose, remember?"

"I should stay in the office and get some paperwork done. And it'll keep Richard off my back about meddling." I shook a finger at her. "As long as you promise to call me as soon as you find out anything."

"I'll come back with a full report," Kate assured me.

Richard emerged from the kitchen with his hands on

his hips. "I would like to lodge a formal protest against this harebrained idea."

"What harebrained idea?" I gave him my most innocent look. "Kate is perfectly capable of gathering information."

"If she comes back with anything more than a stack of men's phone numbers, I'll die of shock."

Kate stood up and slipped her feet into her shoes. "You wait and see what I find out." She grabbed her purse from the floor and marched over to the door. "Sticks and scones may break my bones . . ."

Richard watched as Kate slammed the door behind her and he shook his head slowly. "I rest my case."

Chapter 23

"Have you heard anything from Kate yet?" Leatrice caught me as I tried to stealthily open my mailbox in the building foyer.

"It's barely afternoon." I sighed, looking at my watch. I scooped my mail out of the metal mailbox and snapped the door shut. "She's probably still getting started." Truth be told, she probably just rolled out of bed. Not that I was one to talk. I aspired to make it out of my yoga pants by afternoon. Not that I'd actually made it to yoga class, but I figured getting dressed for it was a step in the right direction. Tomorrow I'd actually attempt a sun salutation.

Leatrice followed me back upstairs. "I've been

thinking about the murders. I think we're missing something."

"Like the killer," I replied absentmindedly as I padded up the stairs in my sock feet. I'd spent the morning printing updated "to-do" lists for clients and returning phone calls. For once my mind was focused on marriage, not murder.

As I reached my landing, I heard my business line ringing. It figured the second I left my desk, the phone would ring. I opened the door and rushed down the hall to get the call in time. I snatched the phone off my desk and steadied my voice. "Wedding Belles. This is Annabelle."

Crap. Nothing but dial tone.

"Did you miss an important call?" Leatrice stood in the hallway behind me, slightly out of breath.

I looked at the caller ID. The Fairmont Hotel. I wondered who could be calling me from there. Hugh the concierge with some juicy gossip? Darcy on the verge of a nervous breakdown? I punched in my voice-mail code.

"Well?" Leatrice rocked back and forth on her heels, making her gold jingle bell necklace ring.

"Isn't that a Christmas necklace?" I asked as I listened to the message.

She gave me a look like I was a simpleton. "On the Style channel they say you should have a signature piece of jewelry, and this is mine."

Somehow I didn't think that was what the Style channel had in mind.

I hung up the phone and put it back on my desk. "They found my car. But it's been scraped up. I'd better grab a cab to the hotel. No way am I calling Richard and having him say 'I told you so' the entire ride there."

"Don't be silly, dear. We can take my car."

I stared at Leatrice for a few seconds. "You have a car?"

"Of course I have a car. I don't drive it much, of course. Not much need when you have everything within walking distance."

"Do you have a license?" I hesitated to ask.

Leatrice gave me a curious look. "Of course. You're not supposed to drive without one, you know."

I didn't dare ask if she'd updated it since the Carter administration. "Okay. Give me a second to get dressed and we can go."

"Perfect." Leatrice clapped her hands. "I'll go warm her up and meet you out front."

I ran into my bedroom as I heard Leatrice close the front door. I tugged on a pair of black pants that I salvaged from the top of the hamper and pulled the plastic dry cleaning bag off a blue silk sweater. I figured the recently cleaned sweater would make up for the not-so-fresh pants. I threw my hair into a ponytail, snatched my black purse from the floor, and headed out the door.

Although the yellow Ford circa 1980 only had four doors, it took up almost as much space as a small stretch limo as it idled loudly in the middle of the

175

street. I didn't see Leatrice at first glance, but I had little doubt that this was her car. They didn't make cars like this anymore. For a reason. I couldn't imagine where in Georgetown she could find a parking space large enough for this monstrosity.

Two loud honks of the car horn made me jump, and I finally noticed Leatrice's jet black hair poking above the steering wheel. "Hop in, dearie."

I opened the passenger door after a few hard tugs and lowered myself into the car. Leatrice perched on a pile of phone books on the driver's side and wore what appeared to be old-fashioned flight goggles and a flying scarf.

She revved the engine. "I feel the need for speed."

Great. Mario Andretti with cataracts. "We're not in any rush," I assured her.

"Don't you want to see what this baby can do? She's in mint condition." Leatrice rubbed the dashboard. "I only take her out for special occasions, but she corners like she's on rails."

"Mint condition" was a slight exaggeration. The fabric roof of the car had started to bubble and sag in places, making the interior seem smaller than it actually was, even though from the outside it looked like we were driving a small apartment. I rolled down my window by hand as Leatrice stuck her arm out the window and merged into traffic.

"Did you just give a hand signal?" I glanced nervously behind me at the car that had slammed on its brakes to let us in.

"The turn signals are on the fritz," Leatrice explained. "Don't worry, though. I know all the hand signals."

I fumbled for my seat belt and wondered if anyone else in the city knew them. My only consolation was that the Fairmont was less than a mile away. How much damage could we do in less than a mile?

Minutes later I pried my fingers off of the armrest and stepped out of the car in front of the Fairmont. Leatrice was indeed the only person in D.C. who knew or used hand signals. At least the official ones.

"That was fun." Leatrice hopped out of the car. She handed her keys to a gawking parking valet and strode after me into the hotel, her long scarf fluttering behind her. "Didn't I tell you she handled like a dream?"

I nodded, still steadying my legs. Driving with Leatrice was like riding in a runaway shopping cart. I paused as we walked into the lobby and noticed every person staring at us.

"Don't you want to take off your goggles, Leatrice?"

She pulled them down so they hung around her neck. "Remind me to put them back on when I drive, though. They're prescription."

"This shouldn't take long. Do you want to wait for me while I talk to the front desk?"

"Wait a second." Her eyes lit up. "This is where the murder took place, isn't it?"

"Yes, but we're not here about the murder. We're here to get my car back, so wait in the lobby and I'll be right—"

"I can't pass up a chance to see the murder scene." Leatrice shook her head. "It would be bad investigating."

"We're not investigating. I promised Richard that I wouldn't poke around and cause any more trouble." I lowered my voice. "There's a killer in the hotel who wasn't too happy that Kate and I were asking questions yesterday and wouldn't be happy to see me snooping around again."

"Then you go find out about your car, and I'll do the poking around." Leatrice headed off across the lobby.

The thought of Leatrice snooping around by herself made me cringe. She was incapable of keeping a low profile, and I feared the mayhem she would create on her own. If I took her, at least I could get her in and out as fast as possible.

I chased after her. "Okay, fine. I'll show you the murder scene, and then we get my car and go."

"Agreed." Leatrice skipped after me as I led the way to the Colonnade.

I hurried down the glass hallway and paused outside the room to listen for any voices before walking in. Silence. I craned my neck around the corner and saw that the room was deserted before waving for Leatrice to follow me inside. The Colonnade was set with a handful of round tables and upholstered chairs but was otherwise bare.

Leatrice went up to the raised gazebo. "Where did you find the body?"

"Over there." I motioned to the far side of the room.

"Now let's get out of here."

"In a minute." Leatrice walked up the stairs of the gazebo and put a hand against one of the large white columns. "So these blocked the view of the murder on the videotape."

"I guess." I walked around to where the ice sculpture had been. "It would be hard to get a clean view across the room with all these columns."

"So even though the chef was killed in broad daylight in a room with glass walls, it would have been difficult to get a good look unless you were in the room." Leatrice tapped her foot while she thought. "Even if someone saw something, it would be hard to distinguish much because of the obstructed view."

"I suppose you're right, but that doesn't tell us anything we don't already know."

"It tells us that the killer knew the room well enough to know where he would be hidden from view," Leatrice said. "Which means that this wasn't a crime of passion. The murder was well-planned. Who arranges the setup of the room?"

"You think the room was arranged for the murder?"

Leatrice shrugged. "Or the killer got very lucky that the ice sculpture sat directly behind a column."

"It must have been a coincidence because Georgia did the room diagram."

"Your friend who was arrested for the murder?" Leatrice raised an eyebrow. "Are you sure she didn't have anything to do with it?"

"Of course I'm sure," I said with more confidence

than I suddenly felt. "She was in jail when the second murder was committed, remember?" I gave myself a mental kick for doubting Georgia.

"What if there are two killers? Didn't you say that one of your suspects is in love with her? Maybe he was her accomplice."

"That's ridiculous. We're leaving, Leatrice." I spun around and my breath caught in my throat. A thin man with sparse dark hair stood in my path. Mr. Elliott.

"You two have some explaining to do," he said without changing his stern expression. "Perhaps I should call Security."

Chapter 24

"Who are you?" Leatrice narrowed her eyes and folded her arms in front of her. I tried not to groan aloud.

"I am the general manager of this hotel." Mr. Elliott looked Leatrice up and down and sneered. His navy suit was perfectly pressed and silver cuff links glinted from his wrists. "Who are you?"

"You're the general manager?" Leatrice looked at me with a glint of recognition. "That's very interesting."

"What I find interesting is what you are doing snooping around my property. Shall I call Security to get some answers?"

"We aren't snooping," I said quickly. "Your hotel

180

lost and damaged my car yesterday, and we're here to pick it up." I returned his sneer. "You should be glad I'm not suing."

"Oh." Mr. Elliott's demeanor changed, and I saw his PR smile for the first time. "I'm terribly sorry."

"You should be," I snapped, building up steam. "I do a lot of business in your hotel, and I don't appreciate having my property damaged."

"Are you one of our frequent guests?" He looked nervous and ran a hand over his perfect hairline. "Perhaps we could make this stay complimentary."

"I'm not a guest. I'm a party planner and I do a lot of events here," I admitted, squinting to get a closer look at the precise rows of hair plugs. Did he really think they looked natural?

"Oh?" He raised his eyebrows. "What kind of events?"

"She's the best wedding planner in town," Leatrice chimed in. "She had a wedding in this room last weekend."

Mr. Elliott studied me more intently. "That was your wedding? I thought you looked familiar." He returned his gaze to Leatrice. "But who are you?"

"I'm her driver." Leatrice tossed her scarf across her neck and over her other shoulder.

"I was just telling my . . . um, driver what a spectacular wedding it was." I shook my head in feigned disappointment. "Such a shame we didn't get any photos before the unfortunate incident. The hotel didn't happen to take any room shots did they?"

Mr. Elliott gave me a curious look. "The hotel? No, we didn't take any pictures of the room."

"I thought you might have arranged for a photographer on your own. For publicity purposes, maybe?" I furrowed my brow as if trying to remember. "I thought someone mentioned something about some room shots being taken."

Mr. Elliott's eyes went cold and hard. "They were mistaken. The hotel had no photos taken. If we had, I'd have known about it."

"Of course. How silly of me. You probably know everything that goes on in your hotel, right?"

Leatrice put her hands on her hips. "Any idea who killed your two chefs, then?"

His jaw muscles flinched. "I'm afraid I'm keeping you from your car. Allow me to escort you to the lobby."

"No need." I breezed by him, waving for Leatrice to follow me. "We have to see Darcy anyway. More business for your hotel."

Leatrice ran to keep up with my pace as we rushed out of the room and down the hallway toward the elevators. "I didn't like that man," she said. "I hope he's high up on your suspect list."

"He is," I assured her. "It's interesting that he denied knowing anything about photos of the room when he used that as his reason to clear the room before the murder."

"Are you sure the source who told you that is reliable?"

"Why would Reg lie?" I brushed off the question. "No, Mr. Elliott is the one with something to hide."

"So there weren't any photos taken?" Leatrice followed me into the open elevator.

"No, but I think he made up the story about having a photographer come in so that everyone would leave the scene of the crime. That would have bought him about five minutes of uninterrupted time during which he could have killed Henri."

"Really?"

I nodded and pressed the button for the second floor. "Because of the setup involved in events, the room is only ready to photograph about ten or fifteen minutes before the guests are invited in. Sometimes we can't even squeeze room shots in because of the tight timing. But if the photographer does have time, it's crucial that the room be cleared so he can get shots without any people in them. Once the staff has been cleared out, they usually don't come back for five or ten minutes."

"So anyone in the event industry would know that?"

"Definitely." I held the elevator door for Leatrice, and then led the way through the glass doors to the executive offices lobby. Beige chairs clustered around a round mahogany coffee table that held sample wedding albums. I smiled at the receptionist sitting behind a narrow wooden desk. "We're here to see Darcy O'Connell, but we don't have an appointment."

"Annabelle?" Darcy poked her head around the

corner. Her hair hung loose around her face and the bags under her eyes seemed to have gotten bigger. She looked like hell. "I thought I heard your voice."

"Darcy, how are you doing?" I asked as diplomatically as possible.

"I'm on my way to check on my cakes for this weekend and get a cup of coffee in the cafeteria. Do you want to join me?" She looked at Leatrice. "What happened to Kate?"

"Oh, we split up today to cover more ground. This is Leatrice."

"I'm her driver." Leatrice stuck out her hand for Darcy to shake.

Darcy shook Leatrice's hand and looked at me. "A driver? I'm in the wrong job."

"She's my neighbor," I explained. "She gave me a ride."

Darcy managed a weak smile and held open the door that led to the back hotel corridors for us. "Should I ask what you're doing back here?"

"This time it's perfectly innocent." I followed Darcy down the wide hallway to the elevators. "Leatrice brought me down to pick up my car since the valets lost it yesterday."

"The valets lost your car?" Darcy looked shocked as she led the way onto an industrial-sized elevator car. "I've heard of them taking a while to bring a car, but not to find it at all?"

"Maybe someone did it on purpose to warn me away from the hotel."

"Like who?" Darcy held the elevator door open for us once we reached the basement.

"Whoever killed Henri and Gunter might not be too thrilled that I was snooping around." I noticed Leatrice lagging behind to read some staff memos tacked to a bulletin board, and I reached back and tugged her forward.

"So, are you any closer to finding out who did it?" Darcy wove her way through the labyrinth of hallways, and I followed closely at her heels, wishing I had bread crumbs to drop behind me.

When we reached the pastry kitchen, Darcy appraised the trays of miniature wedding cakes lined up on a metal counter. Jean looked up from piping icing on them and gave her a curt nod.

"Looks like we're on schedule." Darcy backed out of the narrow entrance to the kitchen.

Leatrice pulled on my sleeve. "Do you mind if I stay behind and watch him work? I've never seen such adorable little cakes."

"Okay, but don't go anywhere," I warned her. "I'll be right upstairs in the employee cafeteria, and I'll come get you in a few minutes."

"Take your time," she called over her shoulder. "This is better than the Cooking channel."

I caught up to Darcy, who held the elevator for me. "Sorry. She doesn't get out much."

"I wish I had her energy," Darcy sighed. The elevator surged up to the second floor, and we got out as a banquet server passed us with a pile of tablecloths.

We passed the dry cleaning counter where all the uniforms were stored and walked into the employee cafeteria.

A few maintenance workers sat at a table in the corner and the TV blared a courtroom drama. Darcy passed the trays of hot food steaming behind glass and made a beeline for the coffee machines. "I don't know how much more of this workload I can take."

"They haven't brought anyone in to help you?" I took the foam cup she offered me and filled it halfway with coffee.

Darcy shook her head. "If Georgia doesn't come back to work soon, I'm a goner. She didn't take great notes, so trying to piece the information together in her files has been a nightmare."

"Georgia was never strong on paperwork, that's for sure." I poured milk into my coffee until it was the color of caramel, then tore open a handful of little blue sweetener packets. "But if everything goes like I hope, Georgia should be released soon."

"Really?" Darcy poured a cup of black coffee and took a sip. "Have you talked to the police?"

"I gave them the video of the murder yesterday, and it shows that the killer is a dark-haired man in a chef's jacket. That should be enough to clear Georgia or at least get them to reconsider other suspects."

Darcy shook her head. "Even if she's released from jail, she might not get to come back to work. I've told you that Mr. Elliott has it in for her."

"That's not fair. He can't fire her because he doesn't

like her. Anyway, I suspect he might have had more to do with the murder than everyone else thinks."

Darcy's eyes bugged out. "You think our GM is a killer?"

"Why not?" I asked. "Everyone thinks he's too spineless to do it, but I think he's every bit ruthless enough to commit murder. Leatrice and I ran into him before we came to see you, and he got very nervous when we brought up the murders."

Darcy went pale. "You talked to Mr. Elliott about the murders? You're braver than I thought."

"Actually, Leatrice brought it up," I admitted.

"Then she's braver than she looks," Darcy said. "Most people in this place are scared of him, including me."

I grinned and glanced at my watch. "Speaking of spunky old ladies, I'd better get her before she drives the pastry chefs crazy."

Darcy looked at the oversized metal clock on the wall. "And I'd better get back to work. No rest for the weary."

We parted ways in the hallway and I traced my steps back to the elevators and down to the pastry kitchen. I stuck my head in the door expecting to hear Leatrice chattering away, but the kitchen was empty. The long metal worktables had pans full of individual square cakes decorated with marzipan fruits, but no sign of Leatrice or any chefs.

Great. She'd probably come looking for me and gotten lost in the maze of hallways.

"I told her to stay put," I grumbled to myself. "Now I'll never find her."

As I turned to leave, my eye recognized a glint of gold on the floor. It looked like one of the jingle bells from Leatrice's necklace. I picked it up and my stomach sank as I saw more scattered on the ground a few feet away.

I had a very bad feeling that Leatrice wasn't wandering in the hallways looking for me. She was in danger.

Chapter 25

"I never should have left her alone with a killer on the loose," I scolded myself, sinking against a narrow metal table. "This is all my fault."

"Talking to ourselves, are we?" The Scottish accent made me jump. "You know that's the first sign of insanity."

"Ian?" I blinked hard. Despite the fact that his extensive arm tattoos were covered up by a black, long-sleeve shirt, he was still hard to miss. "What are you doing here?"

"I happened to be dropping off one of the band's new demos to the catering office and thought I'd say hi to the old gang." He winked at me. "Bit of good luck finding you, I might add."

I sighed with relief that he wasn't stalking me. "Of course. You used to work here."

"In a different lifetime." He grinned. "Before the band made it and I could quit my day job. Would you like to join me for a cup of the world's worst coffee in the employee cafeteria?"

"No." I gave a quick shake of my head, and then saw his face fall. "I mean, I'd love to, but I have to look for my friend, Leatrice. She's missing."

"Your funny little neighbor? Let me help you, then." He pushed up his sleeves to expose part of his tattooed arms. "I know this place inside and out."

"That would be great." I returned his smile. "I left her right here watching the pastry chef about twenty minutes ago. When I came back to get her, she was gone, but I found some little bells from her necklace on the floor."

Ian took the tiny gold bell from my outstretched palm. "These came from a necklace?"

"She likes to wear things that make noise," I explained.

"I don't blame her." Ian grinned at me. A jingle bell necklace was tame in comparison to his stage attire. "Let's look around and see if we can find any more. Maybe they'll lead us in the direction she went."

I dropped down on my hands and knees to get a better view and immediately regretted it. Pastry kitchens weren't known for being spotless. I sat back on my heels and wiped my hands against each other, letting a shower of crumbs fall to the tile floor. At least my black pants hadn't been clean to begin with.

"Any luck?" Ian called from across the room, where

he stood next to an industrial ice cream maker.

I sat back up. "Nothing. Maybe she wandered off looking for me."

Ian came over and held out a hand to pull me up. "She could be lost in the hallways. Odd that neither of us saw her, though."

I took his hand and let myself be hoisted up. "I have a bad feeling that she's in trouble."

"Don't worry." Ian helped me brush off the front of my pants. "How much trouble can you get into in a kitchen?"

I raised an eyebrow at him. "How about being electrocuted or impaled?"

"Right. Forget I said that." He snapped his fingers. "Wait a second. Do you think she could have gotten locked in somewhere accidentally?"

"Like where?" I looked around the room.

Ian pointed at a large metal door by the entrance. "The walk-in freezer. It can be clamped from the outside."

We both rushed over, and Ian yanked on the metal handle and heaved the massive door open.

Leatrice sat on the floor with her aviator's scarf wrapped around her like a mummy and her jingle bell necklace clutched in her hand. My knees felt wobbly seeing her tiny, shivering figure.

I rushed forward. "Are you okay?"

She looked up and smiled weakly. "There you are, dear. I knew you'd find me. I kept ringing my necklace in case you could hear it through the walls."

Ian helped me pull Leatrice up and walk her out of the freezer. He unbuttoned his shirt and slipped it off, revealing a tight black tank top underneath, then draped the shirt around her shoulders.

Leatrice's eyes grew wide as she stared at him, and a little color seeped back into her cheeks. "Oh my. I remember you." She nudged me. "They don't make gentlemen like this anymore, do they, Annabelle?"

I tried to avert my eyes from Ian's naked arms and mostly bare chest. "How did you get locked in there, Leatrice?"

She pulled the shirt closed in front of her. "I watched the chef decorating those precious little cakes, and then he got called out by another chef. I looked around the kitchen while I waited for him to come back. They have amazing gadgets in here, by the way. I didn't even know what half of them were supposed to do."

"The freezer?" I prodded her.

"Right. I was curious about the big metal door, so I opened it and the next thing I knew I was being pushed inside. I tried to resist but I'm afraid I wasn't strong enough. My necklace even got caught on something and it broke in two."

"We found some of them," Ian said. "They must have scattered when they fell."

"Did you see who pushed you?" I asked.

"No. It all happened too fast." She held up her necklace. "Do you think this can be fixed?"

"I'm sure." I patted her on the arm. "I've got super glue in my wedding emergency kit. When we get home, I'll fix it for you."

"You know it's my signature piece," she said.

Ian pulled me back a few steps. "Do you want me to call Security?"

I shook my head. All I wanted to do was go home. It was bad enough that I had Kate out hunting for clues, but I'd never forgive myself if something happened to Leatrice. "I think we've made enough of a stir already without getting Security involved."

"What do you mean?"

"Why else would someone push Leatrice into a freezer if not to warn me off?" I whispered. "We bumped into the general manager and he practically ran us out of the hotel. Clearly people in the hotel know I'm here."

"That Darcy girl knew we were here," Leatrice said, still shivering. "Maybe you shouldn't be so eager to tell her about the investigation, dear."

"Darcy was with me, Leatrice. She doesn't have a reason to kill either chef, anyway." I turned back to Ian. "Someone must have assumed I was here to poke around about the murder, though."

"Why would they assume that?" Ian furrowed his brow.

I avoided his eyes. "Probably because that's what I've been doing the past two times I was here. I promised Georgia that I'd try to find information to clear her of the murder."

Ian let out a low whistle. "That explains a lot."

"But this time I wasn't here to do any investigating,"

I explained. "I came down to get my car, which the parking garage lost yesterday, and Leatrice gave me a ride."

"So this isn't the first mishap you've had here?" Ian asked.

"No, but all I wanted to do was pick up my car. Nobody was even supposed to know I'd been here."

Ian cast a glance at Leatrice, who busily inspected her bell necklace with her prescription goggles. "This is your idea of keeping a low profile?"

"My other options aren't much better."

Ian grinned. "You're right. I've met your assistant and caterer friend. It's a bit of a toss-up, isn't it?"

"Shouldn't we get your car?" Leatrice looked back at us through her goggles. "I feel much better now."

"I don't think you should drive." I shuddered, thinking about Leatrice's driving. I'd hate to see what it was like when she wasn't in peak form.

"But I have to take my car home."

"I'll drive your car home for you," Ian offered.

Leatrice beamed. "Isn't that nice?"

"Are you sure?" I asked. Ian hadn't seen the car yet, and I hesitated to ask if he remembered hand signals.

Ian held out a crooked arm for Leatrice. "It would be my pleasure."

Leatrice giggled and took his arm, then glanced back at me. "Why don't you follow us? I have a feeling we're going to burn rubber."

I sighed. Any chance I ever had to be inconspicuous was officially shot to hell.

Chapter 26

"Where have you been?" Kate lay sprawled out on my couch wearing faded boot-cut jeans and a pink baby doll T-shirt. Her shoes were scattered on the floor and the new issue of Martha Stewart *Weddings* lay open on her lap. "I've been waiting for ages."

When I'd given Kate a key to my apartment for emergency purposes, I hadn't imagined this being one of the disaster scenarios. "I had to get my car from the Fairmont. Leatrice and I ran into some trouble."

"Leatrice?" Kate sat up. "Why would you take her . . . oh, hi, Leatrice."

Leatrice still held tight to Ian's bare arm as they followed me inside. "Kate, dear. Have you met Ian?"

Kate looked at me, then looked at Ian wearing nothing but a tight black tank, and she arched a perfectly penciled eyebrow. "Looks like you had a more exciting day than I did."

Leatrice rushed over to Kate and clutched her arm. "Would you believe that I got locked in a freezer?"

"A freezer? Where were you again?" Kate asked.

Leatrice pulled Kate down on the couch and readjusted Ian's shirt over her shoulders. "I gave Annabelle a ride to the hotel to pick up her car."

"Leatrice insisted on seeing the murder scene," I explained, clearing space on the cluttered dining room table for my purse. "And guess who we ran into while we were there?"

194

"Not a very pleasant man." Leatrice wrinkled her nose. "What was his name?"

"Mr. Elliott," I said.

Kate sat up straight. "You bumped into the general manager? What was he like? Could you tell he had plugs?"

I shuddered. "Like rows of corn."

"That's what that was?" Leatrice shook her head. "I thought he had a condition that made his hair grow funny."

"Mr. Elliott is pretty much like everyone describes him. Not very likable, and even less so when we mentioned the murders," I said. "I don't see why everyone at the hotel thinks he's incapable of murder. He seems the type to me."

"Elliott is a coward." Ian scowled. "He's known for getting other folks to do his dirty work."

Leatrice touched his hand. "Oh, do you know him, dear?"

"We go back a few years," Ian said. "There's no love lost between us, I can assure you."

Ian seemed to have more connections at the Fairmont than I'd realized. I wondered if anyone knew the whole story behind his past there, since he seemed reluctant to share. I made a mental note to ask Richard. He'd forgotten more gossip about the event industry than most people in Washington had ever known.

"So how did you go from the Colonnade room to being locked in a freezer?" Kate asked.

"We ran into Darcy on her way to the cafeteria." I walked over and moved a pile of magazines out of the seat of a chair so I could sit down. "Leatrice got distracted by the pastry chef and stayed with him in the kitchen while Darcy and I grabbed coffee down the hall."

"Let me tell the rest." Leatrice bounced up and down where she sat. "I watched the chef make these adorable miniature cakes. They looked exactly like wedding cakes, only for midgets."

I'd never heard individual wedding cakes explained quite like that before.

"After he left, I stayed behind to look at all of the fancy appliances," Leatrice continued. "The next thing I knew, someone pushed me into the giant freezer and locked the door. If Ian and Annabelle hadn't found me, I'd be a Leatrice-sickle."

"It was Ian's idea to look in the freezer." I smiled at Ian and noticed that his eyes were locked on me. I felt my cheeks flush and looked away. "We're lucky he knows so much about the hotel."

Kate studied Ian for a second. "Lucky you were in the hotel. You're sure you don't still work there?"

"Ian's in a band, Kate." Leatrice smiled. "He told me all about it on the way over here. Apparently the eighties are really hot now. Who knew I was back in style after all these years?"

I decided not to explain the concept of an eighties cover band to Leatrice. It would take way too long.

"We think someone knew we were in the hotel

asking questions and pushed me in as a warning." Leatrice readjusted her aviator scarf around her neck.

I glanced at Leatrice's scarf and goggles and shook my head. "Mr. Elliott, most likely, although I'm sure word got around fast that we were there."

"Or the girl who was asking all the questions about the case," Leatrice said.

"Darcy has been helping us, Leatrice," I explained. "She's on our side, I promise."

Leatrice shrugged. "People can surprise you. Don't you remember that older man with the heavy accent who used to live here? He disappeared only a few days after I saw him on one of those shows about former Nazis who were in hiding."

"He didn't vanish, Leatrice. He moved away. And he was from Russia, not Germany." I turned back to Kate. "So, did you have any luck today?"

"You might say that." Kate stood up and headed to the kitchen. "I'm thirsty. Anyone want anything?"

Leatrice and Ian both shook their heads no. I followed her into the kitchen and stood behind her as she studied the contents of my refrigerator. "Well, are you going to tell me, or what?"

Kate put a finger over her lips. "I'm not so sure we should be telling everyone what we're discovering. First your car disappears, then another chef is murdered, and now Leatrice gets pushed in a freezer? I'm on Richard's side. I don't like the way this is going."

"You're afraid to say anything in front of Leatrice and Ian?" I whispered.

"Not Leatrice, of course. Not that I'd put it past her to create a crime that she could solve." Kate found a can of Diet Coke behind stacks of Chinese take-out cartons and popped it open. "I don't trust Ian. I mean, what do we really know about this guy except that he seems to be at the Fairmont every time we turn around?"

"He did used to work there."

"Exactly my point."

"Not only is Ian the one who helped me find Leatrice, but he doesn't have dark hair." I peeked my head through the opening between the two rooms and saw Leatrice inspecting Ian's tattoos. "He's been nothing but nice since the beginning. I certainly don't believe he has anything to do with the murders. First Leatrice suspects Darcy of being a killer, and now you think Ian might have done it. I think we have enough suspects with real motives to worry about without dreaming up new ones."

"You're probably right. You certainly couldn't mistake that hair for brown, even at a distance."

"I was planning on asking Richard if he knew any gossip about Ian, anyway." I sighed. "Will that make you happy?"

"Good thinking. If he's done anything remotely interesting in the metropolitan area in the past ten years, Richard will know," Kate said. "And you won't see me standing in the way of a possible romance between you and a tattooed rock star who wears a skirt. I wouldn't miss seeing Richard go into cardiac arrest for all the brie in China."

She was right. Richard would have a fit if I started dating Ian. He considered himself the arbiter of my nonexistent love life, and I knew Ian wasn't his idea of a suitable match. Not that he'd approved of any of the would-be suitors I'd tried to scrape up in the past few years.

"Is that the business line ringing?" Kate craned her head around the corner.

"I'll get it." I darted out of the kitchen and down the hall. The phone was only on the third ring when I snatched it off my desk. "Wedding Belles, this is Annabelle."

"Annabelle, it's Detective Reese."

"Detective?" My pulse fluttered, and I steadied my voice. "What did you think of the videotape?"

"Not much. The plastic case was empty."

"What?" I stammered. "That's impossible. I know it was there when I brought it to you. Maybe someone at the station misplaced it."

"Another conspiracy theory?" He laughed harshly. "Listen, Annabelle. I appreciate that you think you're trying to help your friend and that you really believe she's innocent, but I think she'd be better off without your help."

I felt like I'd been punched in the stomach. "But we found evidence that proves she couldn't have been the murderer. It was on that tape. You have to find it."

"We don't have time for a scavenger hunt right now." His voice was firm. "We're running a murder investigation."

"I understand that, but—"

"I don't think you do understand. We've been compiling evidence and testimony, and all of it points to Miss Rhodes."

"But she's being set up," I cried. "Don't you see that? How do you explain another murder at the hotel while she was in custody?"

"We found no evidence that Gunter's death was anything more than an accident."

"Oh, come on." I couldn't keep the irritation out of my voice. "Two deaths in less than a week and you think it's a coincidence?"

"I didn't call you to debate this."

"Then don't let me keep you, Detective," I snapped, and hung up the phone. My hands shook with anger and I felt tears prick the back of my eyes.

"Is everything okay?" Kate peeked around the doorway.

"No." I dropped the phone back on my desk. "That was Detective Reese calling to say that the video wasn't in the case we dropped off and telling me not to waste any more of his time."

Kate's eyes widened. "You're kidding. Our evidence is gone? Now what do we do?"

"Well, the police won't help us. They won't even listen to us anymore." I shrugged. "It's up to us to find the real killer on our own or Georgia's going to prison for murder."

Chapter 27

"Would anyone care to explain to me what those two are doing here?" Richard appeared in the office doorway and jerked a thumb in the direction of Leatrice and Ian in the living room.

Kate jumped. "Don't sneak up on people like that."

"Sorry," Richard said. "The door was open. Leatrice and Ian are debating where she should get her first tattoo, and you're out of your mind if you think I'm going to be a part of that discussion. The idea alone will give me nightmares for weeks."

I glanced at my open desk calendar. "Do we have a meeting I forgot about?"

Richard narrowed his eyes at Kate. "I was summoned for an urgent discussion about some new evidence. I was also instructed to bring empanadas, so this had better be good."

My stomach growled at the sight of the burgeoning white paper bag in Richard's hand. "Are those Julia's Empanadas?"

The hole-in-the-wall empanada shops decorated in neon yellow and red didn't look like much from the outside, but they turned out some of the most decadent savory pastries in the city. I'd developed a serious addiction to the spinach and cheese variety, while Kate loved the one filled with sweet pear. We were lucky they didn't have a shop within walking distance or we'd have to enter a twelve-step program or Weight Watchers.

Richard clutched the bag close. "Yes, but no empanadas for anyone until I know what's going on."

"Yoo-hoo." Leatrice's voice carried down the hallway. "We're going to run downstairs for a second. Ian's never seen a real police scanner before. Anyone want to join us?"

"No, thanks," I called out, sticking my head into the hall. "You two have fun without us."

"Suit yourself, dear." Leatrice had Ian by the hand as she pulled him out the door.

Ian gave me a wink and a helpless shrug as he disappeared from view. I almost felt sorry for him, but better him getting the scanner tutorial than me. Once the door closed, I led Kate and Richard to the living room.

Richard gave my dining room table a cursory glance. "Have you ever actually used this?"

"Don't be ridiculous. Of course I have."

"For dining?" Richard asked.

I stuck my tongue out at him and began clearing the papers off the table. "We can use it now."

Richard dropped the paper bag on the table and disappeared into the kitchen. Once he was out of sight, Kate delved into the bag, pulling out empanadas wrapped in translucent sheets of white paper.

"They're still warm," she moaned.

Richard emerged with a stack of plates, silverware, and paper napkins and began setting the table as I cleaned it off. He pushed Kate out of the way and arranged all the empanadas on a dinner plate in the center of the table, then took a seat at the head.

"Now before anyone takes a bite, I want some explanations," he announced as Kate and I took chairs opposite each other. "Don't think I don't know what's been going on, Annabelle."

I threw my hands in the air. "Nothing has happened with Ian, I swear. Nothing yet, at least. Yes, I agreed to go out with him, but I'm not even sure if we're still on."

"What?" Richard's mouth fell open. "You're seriously considering dating a straight man who owns leather pants? Have I taught you nothing?"

"I can't believe you told Richard," Kate muttered, taking a golden brown empanada from the plate and shaking her head.

"I thought that's what we were talking about." I gulped.

"Well, it is now." Richard shook a finger at me. "I've seen you make some dating blunders, Annabelle, but nothing on this scale before."

"Talk about the pot calling the kettle back," Kate said under her breath.

Richard faced Kate. "Don't even get me started on your dating life. We don't have the time."

"Hey, I'm on your side," Kate said. "I think Ian is all wrong for her."

I picked out a spinach empanada and cut into it, letting the steam escape. "You also think he should be one of our suspects."

"Which is one of the main reasons I think he's all

wrong for you," Kate mumbled through a mouthful of food.

Richard stared at Kate. "Why would he want to kill Henri?"

Kate shrugged. "I haven't worked that part out. It just seems like he happens to turn up whenever Annabelle is at the hotel. Including today when Leatrice coincidentally got locked in a freezer."

"I heard you were at the Fairmont today." Richard shook a finger at me. "I thought you were letting Kate do the snooping from now on."

I didn't bother to ask Richard how he knew. He always had his sources.

"I was," I explained. "But they found my car, and Leatrice was the only person around to give me a ride to the hotel."

"She drives?" Richard gasped.

"Sort of," I said. "Anyway, she ended up getting pushed into a walk-in freezer and Ian helped me find her."

"This is exactly why I said you shouldn't meddle in this murder business anymore." Richard rapped his hand on the table. "I hate being right all the time."

"Don't get all worked up," I said. "Ian found Leatrice before it was too late."

"A knight in shining armor," Richard mused, then looked at Kate. "Convenient."

"You two are impossible. Can't someone be nice?"

"Take it from me, darling." Richard took my hand. "If a man seems too good to be true, it's because he probably is. Remember when I thought I'd found Mr. Right and it turned out he liked to sleep naked holding a ceremonial dagger across his chest?"

Kate nearly choked on her empanada. "I thought I'd had some rough dates."

"If that wasn't bad enough, he kept me up all night playing the lyre. And he was an English professor." Richard shuddered. "Imagine what fetishes a rock singer would have."

"If you know anything about Ian, I'm all ears." I tapped my fingers impatiently on the table. "But I say we should be focusing on the most likely suspects, like the remaining chefs and Mr. Elliott."

Kate snapped her fingers. "The chefs. That's what I wanted to tell you before I got distracted by the empanadas."

"What?" I stopped my fork in midair. "Did you find out something today?"

"You know I had to run by the Willard Hotel to pick up some new catering packets. While I was there, I thought I'd chat with some of the waiters as they set up the ballroom."

"Good thinking, Kate," I said. "Some of those guys have worked there for over twenty years. They probably know a ton about the different chefs who've come and gone."

"And guess who came and went from the Willard?" Kate grinned.

"We already know that Marcello and Henri were sous chefs together there. That's not new."

"But we didn't know that Emilio and Jean were prep cooks at the Willard at the same time."

"You're kidding." I sucked in my breath. "So Marcello knows Emilio and Jean?"

"It would seem so," Kate said. "Talk about a coincidence, huh?"

"Don't tell me you're back on this again," Richard groaned. "How many times do I have to explain to you that my chef was working at the time of the murder? He couldn't possibly have killed Henri."

"Maybe he didn't have to," I said. "Maybe he had an accomplice do the dirty work for him."

"I wonder which one did it." Kate wiped her mouth with a napkin. "We should find out how well Marcello knew each of them."

"Stay away from my chef." Richard stood up and threw his napkin down. "We have a huge party at Evermay tomorrow night, and if you upset him, heads will roll. And when I say heads, I mean yours." He picked up his half-eaten empanada and stormed out the door.

Kate sighed. "By the look on your face, I can tell where we're going after our wedding rehearsal tomorrow night."

"Don't worry," I assured her. "Richard will never know we're there."

"We're going to sneak into a private party, question his chef about his connections to a murder, and then leave without Richard finding out?"

"Exactly," I said, with more confidence than I felt.

Kate put her head in her hands. "One good thing about this plan is that we don't have to worry about the murderer threatening us anymore. Richard is going to kill us first."

Chapter 28

"This is my least favorite part of the job," I complained the next evening as Kate and I waited in the Park Hyatt ballroom for the wedding party to arrive for the rehearsal. After spending the day confirming Nadine's last minute changes with everyone from the cake baker to the string quartet, we'd gotten there early to make sure that the riser and chairs were set up for our mock ceremony. Now I sat in the front row of chairs with a stack of wedding timelines next to me.

The modern ballroom was a long rectangular room in the basement of the hotel decorated in shades of tan and gold. Modern dome-shaped chandeliers dominated the ceiling and provided the only decor. It was a room that adapted nicely to any type of decorations because it was such a neutral palette, but at the moment it looked naked.

"Why is it that everyone is always late for the rehearsal?" Kate sat on the edge of the riser with her legs sprawled in front of her. I said a silent prayer of thanks that she'd chosen a beige pantsuit and not a skirt.

I looked at my watch. The bride had assured me that

everyone would be there at five o'clock, but it was already ten after five and there was no sign of the bride, groom, or anyone remotely resembling a bridesmaid. "They'd better hurry up. We still need to get to Evermay after this."

"I'd hoped you'd forgotten about that." Kate groaned. "I really don't think it's a good idea to provoke Richard when he has a big event. You know how moody he gets."

"I'm telling you, we won't even see Richard. We'll be in and out before he notices us."

"How about I wait in the car? You need a good getaway driver. I can wait on the street with the engine running."

I shook my head. "Nice try."

A woman with fiery orange hair stuck her head in the door. "Is this the Goldman-McIntyre wedding?"

I jumped up. "Yes, you're in the right place."

She opened the door wide and bellowed into the hall, "Harold! I found it."

I motioned for Kate to follow me as I walked to the back of the room. "Are you with the bride's side or the groom's?"

"I'm Doris Goldman, the mother of the groom." The woman with orange hair and equally orange-brown skin held out her hand. Her long fingernails had been painted a metallic copper that miraculously matched her unnatural skin tone exactly, and when she smiled, her teeth almost blinded me. I'd forgotten that the groom was from South Florida until that very moment.

"I'm Annabelle, and this is Kate. We're the wedding planners."

The mother of the groom gave us another brilliant smile. "My husband was right behind me. I'm always losing him." She stuck her head back into the hall and screamed his name again.

"Wonder why?" Kate whispered to me.

A pair of short men, both with thinning hair, came through the door. One leaned on a cane and had less hair than the other.

"We're right here, Doris," the slightly younger man said. "Your father stopped at the water fountain."

"How're ya doing, Dad?" Doris leaned close to her father and shouted into his ear. She turned back to us. "He's legally blind but still gets around like you wouldn't believe."

"Don't fuss over me." He swiped at his daughter with his cane, and then squinted in our direction. "Who are these pretty young fillies?"

Kate gave me a look that said she wasn't fond of being referred to as a filly.

"They're the wedding planners," Doris shouted at a safe distance from the cane.

The grandfather hiked his brown polyester pants even higher around his chest and shuffled over to Kate. He moved pretty fast for a blind guy. "You'll tell me what I need to do, then?"

"Sure." Kate smiled and took a baby step away from him as he slipped a hand around her waist. As his hand drifted south, Kate's eyes widened and she looked to me for help. I bit my lip to keep from laughing.

Doris beamed. "He's quite the ladies' man at his retirement community."

"I can see that," I said.

"Now what's the protocol of escorting single blind grandfathers down the aisle?" Doris rested a hand on my arm.

Did she really think a rule existed for precisely this situation? I imagined flipping through the index of an imaginary wedding protocol book. Grandfathers, blind grandfathers, single blind grandfathers, single blind grandfathers without dates . . .

"There isn't a rule for this, per se—" I began.

"Sorry we're late." Nadine burst through the door with an entourage of bridesmaids scuttling behind her. "We just got out of the salon."

I wondered if the salon had been in Texas, because every girl's hair was teased a mile high. They all wore brightly colored cocktail-length dresses and matching high-heeled sandals, and they were all accessorized out the wazoo. I'd bet money that not a single one of the bridesmaids was from D.C.

Nadine's brown hair had been highlighted with blond streaks and she looked especially tiny in her strapless pink dress with a chocolate brown ribbon belt. I caught the distinctive scent of cigarettes as she approached me, and was surprised not to see one dangling from her fingers.

"Nadine, honey." The mother of the bride followed close on her heels, clutching a huge bouquet of bows and ribbons that were tied onto a paper plate. She wore a pastel blue cocktail suit, a single strand of pearls, and a tortured expression. "Don't forget your stand-in bouquet."

"Let's get this over with." Nadine took the ribbon bouquet from her mother and tossed her pink clutch purse on a nearby chair. "I'm dying for a drink."

Her mother gasped, but the groom's mother tossed her head back and laughed, then walked over and flung an arm around the mother of the bride. "Come on, Audrey. I think we could all use a drink."

The mother of the bride pressed her lips together until they vanished from sight. South Florida meets the Deep South wasn't going too well.

"We probably should wait until David arrives," I said to Nadine, who gave me a blank look. "You know, your fiancé."

She looked around the room and her expression darkened. "Where is he?" She tapped the toe of her pink and brown sandal on the carpet. "He'd better not ruin my wedding."

"We can go ahead and put your bridesmaids in order on the stage," I said to pacify her. "That way when the guys arrive, we'll be ready to do the run-through."

Kate extricated herself from the grandfather's grip and rushed forward. "Let me do it." I'd never seen her so eager to arrange bridesmaids. Usually it was the worst task. Either the girls were too busy gossiping and giggling to listen to our instructions or they thought they knew it all and couldn't be bothered to pay attention. Worse yet were the ones who secretly wanted to be wedding planners and tried to take over. Give me a bunch of clueless guys any day.

"Bridesmaids, follow me," Kate called out as she marched down the aisle toward the stage. The grandfather hobbled forward after Kate, and the girls straggled behind in clusters of twos and threes.

"I hope this doesn't take too long." Nadine sighed, following her bridesmaids. "We need to be at the Occidental Grill by six."

Bold words from a girl who'd breezed in twenty minutes late from the hair salon. I took a deep breath and reminded myself that I hadn't gotten my final payment yet. Be nice, Annabelle.

"I'm worried about her." The mother of the bride came up next to me, her Southern drawl dripping like molasses off every word. "Nadine has always been such a sensitive girl. I think this wedding stress is taking a toll on her nerves."

I looked up at the stage where Nadine stood with one hip jutted out and her hands planted firmly on her hips. Her mother clearly lived in a fantasy world.

"The hard part is almost over," I assured her with one of my meaningless platitudes saved exactly for such an occasion.

"Not that his family has helped matters." She cut her eyes to the groom's family. "They don't care at all about the proper way to do things. It's been most upsetting for poor Nadine."

Poor Nadine chose that moment to bellow across the

room. "Mother, do you have the programs that I asked you to bring?"

"Of course, honey." Her mother hurried forward, taking tiny steps and holding out a Crane's shopping bag. "They're right here."

The mother of the groom sidled up next to me and said in a stage whisper, "That woman needs a laxative worse than anyone I've ever seen."

The mother of the bride twitched in mid-walk, but didn't break her stride or her smile. Despite the fact that the groom's mother was brazen, not to mention completely orange, she was starting to grow on me.

I looked up at the stage where Kate had the bridesmaids arranged in an angled line. Nadine stood glaring at her watch, while her mother began handing out programs. I looked at the ballroom doors and tried to will the groom to appear.

My attempt at mental telepathy was interrupted when the mother of the bride shrieked from the front of the room. I spun around and was thankful to see that she appeared to be fine, although her face was flushed red and her lips were set in a white line. The groom's grandfather stood next to her grinning from ear to ear. For a blind guy with a cane, he sure got around.

"That means he likes you, Audrey," the mother of the groom called out, then threw her head back and laughed.

The bride's mother turned an unpleasant shade of purple and stalked out of the room with the groom's grandfather shuffling after her. At this rate we'd all be lucky to make it to the wedding day.

The groom rushed in the door past his future mother-in-law, followed by a group of large groomsmen.

"Where have you been?" screamed the bride.

The groom looked flushed under his tan, and I could see beads of sweat on his brow as he passed me. "The streets are blocked. There are police cars and ambulances everywhere. We had to park six blocks away and walk."

"What are you talking about?" Nadine's eyes flashed with impatience.

"It's true, Nadine." A groomsman with no neck spoke up in defense of the groom. "Something happened at the hotel across the street. It's nuts out there."

Kate and I looked at each other. There were two hotels that could be considered to be across the street from the Park Hyatt. The Fairmont and the Westin Grand.

"Which hotel?" I asked, my voice barely above a squeak.

"The big one," Neckless said. "I think it starts with an F."

That's what I was afraid of.

214

Chapter 29

"This is a nightmare." Mack lurched toward me on the sidewalk in front of the Park Hyatt dragging a large wrought-iron flower stand behind him.

I tore my attention away from the swarm of police and emergency vehicles across the street at the Fairmont. I hadn't expected to see the Mighty Morphin Flower Arrangers until the wedding day. "What are you doing here?"

"The hotel said we could load in the heavy things tonight to save us some setup time tomorrow." Mack wiped his forehead with a Bikers for Jesus bandana, and then jammed it back in the pocket of his black leather pants. "But if we'd known the streets were going to be closed we never would've bothered."

"Where's Buster?" Kate looked around.

"He's somewhere behind me with the top of the chuppah." Mack sagged against the iron stand, his face flushed pink. I guess black leather didn't breathe very well. "I lost him at a cross walk."

"You just missed Nadine," I said. "The wedding party walked down the street to catch cabs to the rehearsal dinner."

Mack darted his eyes around him. "That was a close one. I don't know if I could handle the Southern belle from hell right now."

"She's nothing," Kate said. "Wait until you see the mother of the groom."

215

"Bad?" Mack asked.

Kate shook her head. "Orange."

"There's Buster." I pointed at the approaching florist, who looked like a football linebacker who'd gotten lost in a leather bar. He carried the top of the iron chuppah frame over his head and people scurried out of the way as he approached.

"I should have known this wedding was going to be a disaster from start to finish." He lowered the iron canopy to the ground with a thud. "If we have to rewrite the proposal more than twice, it always means trouble."

"How many rewrites did Nadine ask for?" I'd lost count months ago.

"Eight." Mack didn't smile. "You know that means we're in for wedding Armageddon."

I sighed and glanced across the street at the swarming police cars and ambulances. "Looks like you might be right."

"Don't tell me there's more trouble at the Fairmont." Buster shook his head. "What else could possibly go wrong?"

Kate shrugged. "We just came outside when you walked up. But whatever happened, it must be serious."

"Speaking of serious, did you have any luck finding out who might have killed the chef?" Mack asked.

"Yes, and no," I admitted. "We have some suspects, but we can't prove anything yet."

"Did you have any luck sending flowers to Georgia?" Kate asked.

Mack frowned. "No. But we did the next best thing."

"We sent her our lawyer," Buster chimed in. "If anyone can get her acquitted, he can."

"I didn't know you had criminal lawyers on your payroll," I said. These guys were full of surprises.

"We had a few unfortunate legal misunderstandings in the past." Buster looked at the ground and cleared his throat. "People see leather and motorcycles and think the worst."

"We haven't actually used him in years, but we keep his office full of flowers," Mack explained. "It's good for business. We've done lots of junior associate weddings from his firm."

"The guy is a pit bull," Buster said. "He thinks he'll have her released any day now."

"That's great." Kate sounded relieved. "We haven't been able to prove anything yet, and our witnesses and evidence keep disappearing."

Mack gave a dismissive wave of the hand. "Don't worry. A really good lawyer doesn't need either."

I gulped. So much for the triumph of justice and the legal system.

"Well, we'd better get this stuff in the ballroom." Buster lifted the iron canopy above his head. "There's more where this came from, and I don't want to be here all night. See you tomorrow, girls."

"And we'll come bearing monkey balls." Mack grinned and followed Buster, dragging the wrought-iron stand behind him.

Kate rubbed her hands together with a wicked glint in her eyes. "I can't wait to see that bouquet."

"Me, too . . . hey, is that Reg running over here?" I squinted across the street.

The banquet captain hurried toward us, looking back over his shoulder several times. His white shirt hung out the front of his pants and his tuxedo jacket looked like it had been slept in. He scooted behind one of the Park Hyatt's thin columns and motioned for us to join him.

"Reg, what are you doing over here?" I asked as we ducked behind the column.

"Forget that," Kate said impatiently. "What's going on over there?"

Reg took a breath. "Emilio is d-d-dead. Frozen to death."

"The chef?" I asked. "How?"

Kate's face fell. "What a shame. He was cute, too."

"They found him locked in one of the walk-in freezers. He'd b-b-been there for hours and the temperature had been turned as low as it could go."

I felt light-headed when I thought of Leatrice's narrow escape from the freezer. "That's horrible. Do they have any idea how it happened?"

Reg pressed his lips together. "The hotel is t-t-trying to say that he locked himself in accidentally, but that's impossible. Emilio was too clever for that."

"They're probably trying to do damage control." I shook my head. "Accidental death sounds better than murder."

Kate shuddered. "Not much better. Who wants to stay at a hotel where the employees keep accidentally killing themselves? Doesn't inspire much confidence in the staff."

I had to agree with Kate's twisted logic.

"The p-police are questioning everyone." Reg chewed on his thumbnail and glanced around the column at the police cars. "I don't think I can take much more of this."

"Calm down, Reg." I patted him on the arm. "You have nothing to worry about."

"Except for being the next victim," Kate said.

I elbowed her in the ribs and looked back at Reg, who'd gotten a few shades paler. "She's kidding. Ignore her."

Kate rubbed her side and glared at me.

"She's right." Reg jerked his head in Kate's direction. "All the victims were in the Colonnade around the time Henri was killed. Maybe someone is killing off any potential witnesses. That would include me."

"Maybe you should tell the police what you know about the general manager," I said. "He's one of the few suspects left and he had plenty of opportunity when he cleared the room for room shots."

Reg darted his eyes to the ground. "About th-th-that—"

"If there's a chance that Mr. Elliot is the killer, you have to tell the police what you know," I insisted.

Reg buried his face in his hands. "I made it all up."

"What?" Kate and I said in unison.

"The story about Mr. Elliot." Reg peeked at us between his fingers. "I made it up so he would look bad. It never happened. He never even mentioned room shots."

My mouth dropped open. "I don't understand."

"I had to do something to help Georgia." He lowered his hands slowly from his face. "Mr. Elliot had it in for her and wanted to fire her even if she was proven innocent. I thought if I could get him arrested for the murder, she'd go free and get her job back."

"So Mr. Elliot wasn't in the room alone?" I asked.

Reg shook his head. "He took one look at the setup and left. I followed him out and went to check on the cocktail party."

"So much for Mr. Elliot being a suspect." Kate sighed. "What a shame. I really despised him."

"I'm sorry." Reg hung his head. "I've made a mess of everything."

"It's okay. You were only trying to help Georgia." I wondered if Georgia had any idea that the shy banquet captain was in love with her.

"She doesn't deserve to be in jail," Reg said firmly. He looked around the column toward the Fairmont. "I had to come tell you the truth, but I'd better get back before I'm missed."

Kate and I watched him scurry back across the street and dart between police cars to enter the hotel.

"I can't believe he made up that whole story." I didn't know whether to be impressed that he went to such lengths for Georgia or angry that he'd led us

220

down the wrong path.

"It was pretty convincing, too." Kate nodded. "I didn't know he had it in him."

"I wonder how many other people are lying to us."

"You mean of the suspects who are still alive?" Kate put her hands on her hips. "We're down two more suspects. Who does that leave at the Fairmont?"

"Well, we still have Jean St. Jean."

"For now." Kate rolled her eyes. "Until he accidentally flambés himself."

"We have another suspect who isn't at the hotel." I started walking toward my car and motioned for Kate to follow me.

"Ian?" Kate asked.

I gave her a dirty look. "No, Miss Smarty Pants. Marcello. I think now is the perfect time to find out what he knows and how involved he is in this whole thing. Come on. We have a party at Evermay to go to."

"If Richard catches us, it's not going to be pretty," Kate reminded me.

"Don't worry." I hunted in my purse for my car keys. "Your workman's comp is all paid up."

Kate gave me a sugary smile. "How comforting."

"How many times do I have to tell you?" I said. "He'll never know we were there. You should be more worried about the fact that a killer is still on the loose."

"Between an unknown murderer and Richard when he gets in a foul mood?" Kate muttered. "I'll take my chances with the serial killer."

Chapter 30

"Are you sure it's okay to leave the car here?" Kate asked as I drove up Evermay's steep drive and parked in front of the caretaker's house across from the mansion. "Can't Richard see the car from the front door?"

"I'm sure he's too busy to come outside." I glanced at my watch. "The party starts in half an hour, so he's probably torturing waiters right about now."

"Maybe I should wait with the car in case the valets need us to move it."

"Nice try, but let's go." I stepped out of the car and waited for Kate to join me. "Look at it this way. The faster we get in and talk to Marcello, the faster we can get out."

"Then what are we waiting for?" Kate tugged me by the sleeve as she marched up the historic house's circular drive.

We passed the enormous round marble fountain that dominated the entrance, and I paused to look up at the house. The red brick mansion was classic in design, but nonetheless imposing. Long rectangular windows were stacked in orderly rows across the front of the house and draped with heavy curtains inside. Wings had been added to each end of the square building, softening its edges.

I followed Kate up to the large wooden front door, and we peeked in the side glass panels. No sign of

Richard. I turned the brass handle and slowly pushed the door open.

"He's probably in the tent on the other side of the house," I whispered to Kate, waving her into the elongated foyer.

"You didn't tell me my hair was a mess." Kate examined her short blond bob in the large mirror that hung on the wall.

I closed the door gingerly. "You look fine. It's not like we're going to see any eligible bachelors while we're here."

"You never know." Kate wagged a finger at me. "Always be prepared."

Somehow I didn't think this was what the Boy Scouts had in mind when they chose their motto. I led the way through the formal dining room to the kitchen, pausing at the swinging door to the kitchen, and listened to the familiar baritone.

Kate raised an eyebrow. "Is that the theme song to *The Dukes of Hazzard*?"

"I think so." I'd never heard an operatic version of the song so it was hard to tell.

Kate rolled her eyes. "Richard sure knows how to pick them."

I put a finger to my lips. "Follow my lead."

I pushed open the kitchen door and ran straight into a stack of plastic glass racks that reached my chest. I edged my way around them, trying not to trip on the heavy plastic sheeting that covered the floor. Marcello stood with his back to us at the counter of the long, narrow galley kitchen.

"The hors d'oeuvres aren't ready yet," he bellowed. "Come back in ten minutes and not a moment sooner."

I cleared my throat. "We wanted to say hello before the event began."

Marcello spun around, and his expression changed from irritation to surprise. "You two. Richard didn't tell me this was your event."

"You know Richard when he gets caught up in things," Kate said with a nervous giggle. "Probably slipped his mind."

Marcello nodded and turned back to his chopping board. "You must excuse me. We're running behind schedule. One of the delivery trucks ran out of gas on the way so the food arrived an hour late."

I groaned. Nothing made Richard more frantic than running late during setup. He would be beyond hysterical, and I knew from experience it wasn't a pretty sight.

"Let's go before he finds us here," Kate said under her breath. She knew Richard as well as I did.

I shook my head and took a step toward Marcello. "Did you hear what happened at the Fairmont tonight?" I tried to sound as casual as possible.

Marcello hesitated for a second before he continued chopping. "Something else happened?"

"Another accidental death," I continued. "The chefs there seem to be very careless."

"A chef?" He held his knife in midair above the counter. "Who?"

"Emilio," I said. "Locked himself in a walk-in freezer."

Marcello lowered his knife slowly and leaned against the counter with both hands. I noticed his fingers turning white from the pressure. So he really didn't know about the murder after all.

"Didn't you know him?" Kate asked.

Marcello gave an abrupt nod, and then picked up his knife again. "We were colleagues once. In this business you work with everyone at some point."

"I thought he worked under you and Henri when you were sous chefs at the Willard," I said. "So did Jean St. Jean, right?"

Marcello shrugged, but the back of his neck reddened. "Like I said, I've worked with almost everyone in this town."

From his reaction, I'd say he knew Emilio a little better than he claimed to.

"You must admit that it's somewhat of a coincidence for two of your former employees to have worked under Henri, the man you despised, who's now dead." I braced myself for an angry response.

Marcello turned around and began laughing softly. "You think I had something to do with Henri's death? And perhaps the two sous chefs as well?"

"I'm sure Annabelle didn't mean to imply—" Kate began, taking a baby step back.

"I was nowhere near the hotel when Henri was killed, and I have a kitchen full of cooks to prove it, so you'd better come up with something better than a coincidence if you plan to accuse me of murder."

I swallowed hard and put on my best poker face. "You didn't have to actually kill Henri if you master-minded the whole thing. I think you convinced one of your former colleagues, who hated Henri as much as you, to do the deed."

Marcello arched an eyebrow and leaned in toward me. "Interesting idea, but why would someone commit murder for me? I'm afraid my colleagues aren't that loyal. Your theory has a few holes in it, Miss Wedding Planner."

So much for my visions of a spontaneous murder confession à la Perry Mason. Marcello actually made a good point. Why would someone commit murder for someone else? I knew I had the pieces to this murder puzzle in front of me, but I couldn't manage to put them together.

"Oh, well. You can't blame a girl for trying," Kate said a little too brightly. "Let's go, Annabelle."

I gave her a withering look.

"Where are my hors d'oeuvres?" Richard's shrill voice carried into the kitchen from the door that led onto the back terrace. He was headed right for us.

"We'd better let you get back to those hors d'oeuvres." I nudged Kate toward the kitchen door. "Richard hates it when food is late."

I caught one final glance of the seething chef before exiting the kitchen and hurrying into the dining room.

"Well that got us nowhere," Kate grumbled.

"Everyone needs to be dressed in five minutes,

people." Richard's voice echoed from the foyer. "If I see so much as one T-shirt, heads will roll."

Kate clutched my arm. "He's right outside the room. He must have come through the foyer's door to the terrace. What do we do?"

I turned back to the kitchen, but Kate shook her head.

"I'm not going back in there," she said. "He'll kill us, or worse, turn us over to Richard."

I looked around the sparse formal dining room for a place to hide. Asian art covered the soft green walls and a large wooden table took up the center of the room. I peered up at the crystal chandelier that burned real wax candles. No help there.

"Great," Kate whimpered. "Not even a couch to cower behind."

I eyed the large painted screen that was pressed up against the back wall. "We can hide behind that. Follow me."

We carefully shimmied the screen away from the wall far enough to slide behind it just as we heard Richard's rapid-fire footsteps enter the room. I held my breath as he walked past us. From the corner of my eye I could see him barrel into the kitchen. I let out my breath as I heard the cacophony of Richard's shrieks and Marcello's booming replies.

"We'd better make a run for it," I said.

"I'm not going anywhere with Richard on the warpath like that. I'm perfectly fine right here, thank you."

"Kate, we can't stay here the entire event. Guests are going to start arriving soon. One of them is bound to see us like this."

"As soon as we step out from behind here, Richard's going to walk out. I know it," Kate whispered. "Why don't we walk behind the screen until we get close enough to the door to make a run for it?"

"You're kidding, right?" I rolled my eyes. "You don't think a screen lurching across the room on its own will attract attention?"

"We'll go slowly and stick close to the wall." Kate edged her side of the screen over. "Work with me, Annabelle."

"Oh for God's sake," I muttered, pushing my end out with my foot. "I'll bet other wedding planners don't do this type of thing."

"We've always wanted to be unique." Kate shuffled sideways. "I think this would qualify."

"Oh, shut up."

We ambled the screen around the outskirts of the dining room until we were almost at the door. I poked my head out and looked into the foyer.

"The coast is clear." I waved for Kate to follow me. "It's now or never."

We abandoned the screen and scurried through the foyer and out the front door. I pulled the heavy door behind me as silently as possible and jumped when I heard Richard's voice on the other side.

"Who moved this screen? Anyone? It couldn't have walked over here by itself, people. When I find out who's responsible . . ."

I started running with Kate close at my heels, and we were both breathing hard when we reached the car. I cast a glance over my shoulder and sighed in relief. No Richard.

"Good thing he didn't see us." I felt a twinge of guilt. "I feel sorry for the poor person who has to suffer his wrath for moving the screen."

"Tell me about it." Kate collapsed against the passenger side. "When he gets his feathers muffled, there's no living with him."

Chapter 31

"I'd call last night a total bomb." Kate collapsed onto my couch, draping her arm across her eyes. From what I could see, her black suit reached her knee and didn't show any cleavage. I studied her carefully for a hidden side slit or peekaboo back. Nothing. Either everything she owned was at the dry cleaner or she'd finally decided to dress appropriately for a wedding.

"I wouldn't say that." I tucked in my ivory silk shell and zipped up the side of my black dress pants.

"You didn't miss a date with the cutest new senatorial staffer."

"You had a date last night?" I didn't know why I was so surprised. When it came to her social life, Kate was a champion multitasker.

"We were supposed to have dinner at Ceiba, but

after the covert mission you dragged me on I was too wiped out to go home, put together an irresistibly cute outfit, and be captivating for a few hours." She peeked at me from under her arm. "I really could have used one of their mojitos, too."

"Our covert mission, as you call it, wasn't a total waste of time." I pulled back my living room curtains and squinted at the bright sunshine, crossing my fingers for some clouds before our outdoor photo session with the bride. Every bride prayed for sunny weather, but photos were more flattering when it was slightly overcast.

"How do you figure that?"

"Didn't you see Marcello's reaction when we accused him of being an accomplice to murder?"

"First off, *we* didn't accuse him of being involved in the murder. That was all you." Kate shook her head. "Personally, I never tick off someone holding a knife."

"Don't you think he was awfully calm about the whole thing?" I hoisted my metal emergency kit onto the table and opened it to see if I needed to restock any wedding supplies.

"Maybe because he didn't do it?"

"I know we can't prove anything, but I just have a feeling that he's involved. Everyone else hated Henri because he was horrible, but Marcello had a real motive. He lost his career, his wife, his kid."

"It's not like he talks about them, though." Kate sat up and adjusted the waist of her black panty hose. "Maybe his wife would have left him anyway. He does have a nasty temper."

I pawed through the contents of my wedding "crash" kit, as Kate lovingly called it. Safety pins, bobby pins, ink pens, hair spray, bug spray, static guard, fake rings, scissors, tape, glue, white-out, sewing kit, buttons, Velcro, ribbon, powder, chalk, extra strength aspirin. We were in business.

"I still have a feeling that Marcello knows something, even if he didn't actually do it," I said.

"Since the police lost our only real evidence, we might never know who did it."

I groaned. "Don't remind me."

"At least Joni hasn't asked for her tape back yet. If we're lucky, the bride won't even want to see her video." Kate gave a small shudder. "Would you want to relive that?"

"Wait a second." I closed the emergency kit quickly and fastened the metal clasps. "Why didn't I think about this before?"

"What? Why do you have that look like you're up to something?"

"I'll bet Joni didn't give us her only copy of the footage. She always copies weddings onto her hard drive so she can edit them, and I'm sure she makes backups."

"You mean in case the wedding planners borrow them and give them to the police as evidence in a murder case?" Kate didn't sound convinced.

"Exactly." I grabbed the phone off the coffee table and dialed the videographer's phone number from memory. Answering machine. I left a long message explaining everything and gave her my cell phone number.

"Anyone home?" Leatrice cooed as she pushed open the door.

I glared at Kate as I put the phone back on its charger. "You didn't close the door behind you?"

"Sorry." She winced. "We're just about to leave for a wedding, Leatrice."

"Lucky I came up when I did." Leatrice bounced into the room wearing a multicolored sweater with three-dimensional puffy penguins sewn all over it. "Ian and I have a theory about the murders that I wanted to share with you."

"You and Ian?" I looked at the door. "He's here, too?"

"Not now." Leatrice laughed. "But he was here last night looking for you. I told him you must be out working so I invited him in and we had TV dinners together."

Kate frowned at me. "Did you stand him up?"

My mouth went dry as I vaguely recalled a previous mention of a Friday night date. Had I missed my only real date in months? "I don't think so. At least I don't remember setting a definite time."

"You need some serious help, Annabelle." Kate gave me an exasperated sigh. "I see that I'm going to have to put some overtime in to bring you up to speed on dating."

"Can I help?" Leatrice clapped her hands.

Just what I needed. Dating advice from an eighty-year-old in a three-dimensional penguin sweater. I'd have to call Ian later and try to explain, but for now I had to focus on the murder. Not to mention the wedding.

"What's your theory, Leatrice?" I tried to change the subject.

Her eyes lit up. "Ian thinks that it had to be Mr. Elliott, and I have to agree that he's a completely unpleasant man."

"We've been down this road before." I slipped my black suit jacket off the back of a dining room chair. "As much as I'd love him to be guilty, I just don't think he has the motive."

"Did Ian tell you why he's convinced the GM did it?" Kate asked.

"He seems to know everyone at the hotel pretty well. I guess he thinks Mr. Elliott is the most likely person to commit murder." Leatrice blushed. "He's such a nice boy once you get past the tattoos. He even promised to come over and help me with some surveillance this afternoon. Too bad you girls have to go. I'm going to heat up frozen corn dogs."

Poor Ian. This had to be one of his tamer Saturdays.

"What type of surveillance?" I hesitated to ask.

Leatrice lowered her voice and darted a glance over her shoulder. "You know that couple that moved into the second-floor apartment?"

I nodded. "The ones from California?"

"Or so they say." Leatrice gave us a knowing look.

233

"I think they're really moles."

"What?" Kate stifled a laugh.

"Sleeper spies," Leatrice continued. "They're planted here by foreign governments and they wait until the perfect moment to spring into action. I've been observing them for weeks."

"No wonder this building has so much turnover," Kate said under her breath.

"You know that Washington has more spies than any other place in the world, don't you?" Leatrice didn't wait for an answer. "We have to stay on our toes, girls."

"Sorry we're going to miss all the fun, but we have to run or we'll be late." I slipped on my jacket and grabbed my emergency kit off the table. "Tell Ian that I said hi and that I didn't mean to stand him up. It's just that I didn't remember . . . no, don't tell him that. I didn't know we had a date . . . no, that doesn't sound good, either. . . ."

"Don't worry, dear." Leatrice squeezed my hand. "I'll explain that you've been a bit frazzled what with work and the murders."

Exactly what a man wanted to hear. "Thanks, Leatrice."

She followed us out the door and waved as we hurried down the stairs.

Once we were out of earshot, Kate turned to me. "I hate to be the one to tell you, Annabelle, but she's nuttier than a fruit bake."

Chapter 32

"I hope you know that I cannot work under these conditions, Annabelle." Fern clutched my arm as Kate and I entered the bride's suite at the Park Hyatt Hotel. His sunflower yellow shirt was unbuttoned at the collar and his sleeves were rolled up to the elbow. He tapped a round hairbrush nervously in the palm of his hand.

"What now?" I dropped my heavy emergency kit on the floor and sized him up. I'd never seen him so informal or so frazzled.

"Fern!" Nadine bellowed from where she sat across the room by the window. "I'm ready to try again."

"I've already done three updos and she's ripped out every single one." He wrung his ring-laden hands. "I haven't even started on the bridesmaids, and they're all supposed to be ready for pictures in two hours."

I looked at the sullen bridesmaids who sat around the room on plush taupe furniture, silently nibbling on muffins and watching the Weather channel. The dining room table was filled from end to end with trays of fruit and baskets of bagels that looked severely picked over. Celedon green bridesmaid dresses hung off the backs of doors and over chairs, and duffel bags were scattered around the floor. A typical prewedding scene.

"Didn't you do a trial?" Kate asked.

"Two." Fern shot a menacing look over his shoulder at the bride. "But apparently she's been pulling out magazine pictures of other styles since then."

I cringed. If Nadine was as indecisive about her hair as she had been about everything else with the wedding planning, we'd never get her down the aisle.

"How I am supposed to do this?" Fern waved a glossy magazine page in front of us. The bride in the photo had her hair teased up about half a mile, with a snake winding its way around her shoulders and through the top of the hairdo. "Unless you happen to carry a spare snake?"

"Do you want me to check, Annie?" Kate motioned to the emergency kit, and then pressed her lips together to keep from laughing.

"I'm waiting," Nadine called in a singsong voice that bristled with impatience.

"I wish I did have a snake," Fern muttered.

"I think what we need is a change of atmosphere." I picked up the phone on the wooden end table, dialed room service and ordered three bottles of champagne. I turned off the television and turned on the stereo, adjusting the dial to a hip-hop station. "All right, ladies, champagne is on the way, so why don't we start the celebration a little early?" The room quickly filled with excited chatter.

"Not bad." Fern gave me an appreciative nod. "I'd better get back to work. Let me know if you make any headway on the snake."

"This is quite a change." Kate smirked at me. "Usually you're warning brides not to drink so much on the wedding day."

"In this case I think it might help." I heard the muffled ringing of my cell phone and dug into my purse. I crossed my fingers that it wasn't another wedding crisis as I flipped the phone open. "This is Annabelle."

"It's me. You're not going to believe what I found."

"Me who?" I asked, pressing the phone closer to my ear so I could hear over the giggling of the bridesmaids.

"Joni," she said breathlessly. "I'm watching the tape of last week's wedding again."

I let out a long sigh. "So you made a copy?"

"Of course I made a copy. You think I'd give away my master?"

"Well, no." I felt silly. "So, what did you find?"

"I got this new editing system last week. It's the latest thing on the market. You'd kill me if you knew how much it cost, but anyway, it's the top of the line and it has tons of new features. No one else in town has anything close to this—"

"Does this have something to do with the tape?" I tried not to sound impatient.

"I'm getting to it." She took a quick breath and then continued. "So I was playing around with some of the new features. You know, getting to know the system. When I heard your message, I thought that I'd put the footage on the new system and see what it could do."

"And?" I urged her on.

"By using the new zoom feature, I was able to home in on the figure that comes into the room with the chef that was killed. I cleaned up the image and focused on the names on the jackets."

"That's brilliant." I held my breath. "So you know the name of the killer?"

"Actually, the *names* of the killers," she said. "Plural."

"What?" I held tight to the phone to keep from dropping it.

"That's right. Three different dark-haired men had a part in killing the chef. I wrote their names down. Gunter, Emilio, and Jean."

"Oh my God." I could barely breathe. "They all did it. Jean must have gotten rid of his accomplices in case they decided to turn on him."

"What?" Joni asked. "You're breaking up a little."

"Nothing." I had to get off the phone so I could call Reese. "I've got to run. This is great, Joni. Thanks for everything."

"Don't mention it. I'm glad I decided to spring for the new system. I'll be paying it off forever, but you should see the things it can do—"

"I'm losing you. I'm going through a tunnel." I snapped the phone shut and turned to Kate, who was perched on the arm of the couch reading the wedding schedule.

She glanced up at me and did a double take. "You're white as a sheet. What's the matter? Is the photographer stuck in traffic?"

"That was Joni on the phone. She had a copy of the video and used some new system she got to zoom in and read the names of the killers on their jackets."

"Killers?"

"Gunter, Emilio, and Jean. They all did it."

"Tag team murder?" Kate's hand flew to her mouth. "No way."

"Way," I said, and flipped open my phone again. "I have to call Reese and tell him."

Kate shook her head. "So Jean killed everyone, then?"

"He must have." I punched the numbers on the keypad. "Maybe he thought the others would confess or maybe he was on a roll." I counted the rings and wondered if Reese would be working on a Saturday.

"Precinct Two." A clipped woman's voice answered on the fifth ring.

"Detective Reese, please. Tell him it's Annabelle Archer and it's an emergency."

"Hold on." The phone clattered against something, and I heard voices in the background. I guess their phones didn't have hold buttons yet.

"Reese here."

"Detective, this is Annabelle Archer." The words tumbled out of my mouth. "Sorry to bother you on a weekend, but this is urgent."

"It's okay. I'm working, anyway."

"Champagne for everyone!" one of the bridesmaids squealed as a waiter wheeled a cart with silver ice buckets into the room.

"I won't ask what you're doing." He sounded amused.

"I'll have you know I'm at a wedding." I tried to

keep the irritation from creeping into my voice. "But I called you about the Fairmont murder case. I know who killed Henri, and I have solid proof this time."

He sighed. "At this point I'm willing to listen to anything."

"The videographer from the wedding kept a copy of the tape that you lost. She was able to zoom in and read the names off the jackets of the people who were in the room with Henri."

"I'm listening." Now he sounded interested.

"There wasn't one killer. There were three. Gunter, Emilio, and Jean all had a part in killing their boss. It's on the tape." I gasped for air and waited for Reese's reaction.

"So Jean must have gotten rid of his accomplices to make sure they wouldn't turn on him."

"That's what we thought, too. Now you have to release Georgia, right? If we've proved that someone else did it?"

"Georgia? We released her last night. That's one hell of a lawyer she got herself."

"She's free?" I felt a weight lift off my shoulders.

"I've never seen anyone as eager to get back to work as she was. She said she hadn't missed one of her weddings in ten years and she wasn't going to miss the one she had today. People in your business really are obsessive, aren't they?"

A chill rushed over me. "She's going back to the hotel today? But Jean is still there. What if he's the one who set her up for the murder? He's not going to be too happy that she's out. He's already killed three people. What's to stop him from killing another?"

"Calm down, Annabelle," Reese said, but I could hear the edge in his voice. "I'm on my way to the Fairmont right now. Whatever you do, don't go in there without me."

"Then you'd better hurry." I hung up and dialed the Fairmont switchboard with shaking fingers. I asked to be put through to Georgia's office, and I held my breath as the phone rang. My heart sank as my call went into voice mail.

"Georgia, it's Annabelle," I said after the beep. "You're in danger. You have to get out of the hotel right now." I hung up the phone and dropped it in my jacket pocket. Kate caught me as I reached the door.

"Where do you think you're going?"

"Georgia's over there with Jean and she doesn't know that he's the killer. If she's walking around the hotel, she won't get my message in time. I have to warn her."

"Are you insane?" Kate grabbed me by the shoulders. "This guy is dangerous. He's already killed three chefs and tried to kill Leatrice."

"It's okay." I shook loose of her grip. "Reese is meeting me over there. I need you to run things for a few minutes while I'm gone. I'll be back before you know it."

Kate darted her eyes to Nadine, who now wore a beehive and tossed back a glass of champagne in one gulp. Kate's eyes filled with panic. "It's too dangerous

241

over there. I'll go."

"Nice try. You'll be fine here," I said. "You've got Fern to help."

Kate looked at Fern, who brandished a brush in one hand and a bottle of champagne in the other.

"I'm telling you girls." He took a swig of champagne. "Sex is the last thing you'll want on your wedding night. After being on your feet all day and seeing all those people? Not on your life! Take it from an expert."

"Right." Kate raised an eyebrow. "Why was I worried?"

Chapter 33

"Where's Georgia?" I rushed up to the Fairmont's concierge stand, panting from my dash through the Park Hyatt lobby and across the street. "Has she come in yet?"

Hugh jumped when he saw me, then straightened his formal concierge jacket. "Take it easy, Annabelle. I know you're as excited to see her as we all are, but there's no need to—"

"I have to find her," I pleaded. "She could be in danger."

Hugh leaned over his desk. "What kind of danger? Are you sure?"

"I need to find her before she runs into Jean."

"Do you mean that Jean had something to do with

the murder?" Hugh lowered his voice as a guest walked past us.

"I think Jean had something to do with all the deaths in the hotel, and I don't think he'll be too happy that the person he set up to take the fall for killing Henri is free. If he's crazy enough to kill three times, then he's crazy enough to come after Georgia."

"That's such a shame." Hugh shook his head. "He's the best pastry chef we've had in years. I'm going to miss his chocolate decadence cake."

I rolled my eyes. "So have you seen Georgia?"

"She came in a little while ago, but she was running around saying hi to all the departments." Hugh smoothed his moustache with his index finger and looked puzzled. "I don't know where you'll find her, but wherever you do, Reg won't be far behind. He's been following her around like a puppy. Oddly enough, she doesn't seem to mind him. Jail must have had a profound change on her."

"Now that I'd like to see." I grinned at the thought of Georgia reevaluating her life. "Any idea where I should start looking for her, though? I'm not exactly in the mood for a wild goose chase."

Hugh snapped his fingers. "She does have a wedding later today in the Colonnade. I know the tables are down, and Jean was going to start setting up the cake. Apparently it's six tiers and blue."

Blue? Apparently no one wanted a traditional wedding cake anymore.

"So she might be in the Colonnade with Jean? If the

police come, can you tell them where I am?" I didn't wait for Hugh to answer before turning and hurrying across the lobby. I leapt the two steps into the sunken lobby lounge and ran on tiptoes down the marble hallway to the Colonnade so my heels wouldn't announce my arrival. I stopped and caught my breath before entering the room.

The tables were set up and covered with pale blue satin tablecloths, giving the room an icy look. I slowly walked around to where Jean stood with his back to me, assembling a giant blue wedding cake on the baby grand piano. A metal pastry cart on wheels stood beside him with piping tubes and extra bowls of blue icing.

"I am not fond of spectators while I work." He gave me a disdainful glance over his shoulder, and then resumed piping a pearl border on the cake.

I quickly assessed that the pastry cart didn't hold any knives. "I didn't come to watch you work. I came to talk to you about the murders."

"This again?" He sighed impatiently, but continued his work. "I have told you everything."

"You failed to mention that you and your chef buddies conspired to get rid of Henri together, and then you killed off your accomplices."

"Absurd," he spat out. "You think I killed my colleagues? My friends?"

"Henri wasn't your friend."

He slapped his piping tube down next to the cake. "True enough. His death was well-deserved. But I didn't do it."

244

"Not alone, at least," I pressed. "We have evidence that you, Gunter, and Emilio killed Henri together. It was caught on tape."

"I heard about the tape." He turned to face me. "I suppose it was recovered?"

How did he know about the tape? And how did he know it was missing?

"The police have it, and it proves that you were involved," I bluffed. "It's only a matter of time before they find evidence to link you to Gunter's and Emilio's deaths, too."

"I don't have to stand here and be accused of murder." His eyes flashed. "If you'll excuse me, my work here is finished."

I took a step forward. "I can't let you go."

He turned back slowly, one side of his mouth crooked up in a smile. "And what do you intend to do? Subdue me yourself? Arrest me?"

The thought of a citizen's arrest didn't seem realistic at the moment since Jean had a good fifty pounds advantage over me. He fisted his hands and stepped from behind the pastry cart.

"Well, no, but . . ." I stammered.

"I can handle that part," Reese said as he strode into the room, several uniformed officers following behind him. "We're going to need to take you in for questioning regarding the murder of Chef Henri."

Jean arched an eyebrow but didn't move from his spot. An officer grabbed him by the elbow and started to lead him out of the room. He seemed totally uninterested in the process, but his eyes didn't leave mine.

"Don't believe everything you see," Jean said so quietly that I could barely hear him.

"You okay?" Reese asked, waving a hand in front of me.

"I'm fine." I pulled my eyes away from the chef as the officers escorted him away, and I looked up at Reese. "He never really threatened me. As a matter of fact, he seemed more insulted than angry."

"Some people are like that," Reese said. "Not all murderers are raving lunatics."

"Good thing." I smiled weakly. "I have enough raving lunatics for clients."

Reese laughed. "You know you aren't a typical girl, don't you?"

"You mean your blondie doesn't get involved in murder cases?" I said before I thought better of it.

He raised an eyebrow at me and held my gaze with his hazel green eyes. "I didn't know I had a blondie, but no, I don't know any other women who get involved in murder cases."

"Oh." I felt the heat creeping up my neck. "Well, I don't go looking for trouble, you know."

Reese cocked his head to one side. "That's still up for debate."

"I was only trying to help an old friend who was being framed for murder." I put my hands on my hips. "Anyone would have done the same thing."

Reese studied me for a moment, and then gently brushed a loose hair off my face. "I'm not so sure about that. You have lucky friends."

"Thanks." My mouth went dry and I could feel my heart pounding. I only hoped that Reese couldn't hear it, too.

"Now that your friend has been cleared, I hope you'll stay out of my murder investigations." He winked at me. "You drive me a little bit crazy."

"Oh." My heart sank. "Sorry."

"Don't be sorry," Reese leaned in to me and whispered. "It's not a bad crazy."

"Oh." I tried to keep my knees from buckling.

"There you are," Richard called as he stomped into the room in jeans and a white button-down. "I've been looking everywhere for you."

Reese straightened up, and I jumped away from him.

"Richard." I cleared my throat. "What are you doing here?"

"Kate has been calling me nonstop." He waved his cell phone in the air. "Lucky for you I have today off and can swoop in and save the day again." He paused when he saw Reese. "Well, well, it looks like help already arrived."

"Sorry Kate dragged you down here, but everything's fine," I explained. "The police just took Jean away."

"Kate was babbling about Jean St. Jean and a tape and you being in trouble, but I couldn't make any sense of it." Richard crossed his arms in front of him. "So you aren't in grave danger?"

I shook my head. "Actually, Jean went pretty quietly."

"So I drove down here and valet parked for nothing?" Apparently his mood hadn't improved since last night.

"Not for nothing," I said, my mind racing. "Georgia is out of jail and back at work. Do you want to come find her with me and say hi?"

"I suppose so," he grumbled. "So the trip won't have been a total loss."

I turned to Reese. "I'd better go."

"I'm going to tie up a few loose ends around here, and then head back to the station," Reese said. "I'm glad things turned out well for you and for Georgia."

"Me, too." I nodded. I wanted to say something else, but I could feel Richard's eyes on me. "See you later."

"Count on it." Reese winked almost imperceptibly before he strode out of the room.

Richard raised his eyebrows. "I'm not even going to comment on that."

"I don't know what you're talking about," I said in my most innocent voice.

Richard shook a finger at me. "What's that saying about burning the candle at both ends, or is it playing both ends against the middle?"

"Now you sound like Kate." I started to walk out of the Colonnade. "And I still have no idea what you're referring to."

"Don't think I haven't noticed your little flirtation with tattoo boy." Richard followed me. "Although

I've had the good taste to overlook it."

"You're overreacting, as usual."

Richard gasped and stopped in his tracks. "I never overreact."

Classic. Before I could respond, my cell phone began singing, and I reached into my pocket to retrieve it. I looked on the caller ID before answering.

"Hi, Kate," I said as I flipped it open. "Everything's fine. They took Jean away for questioning."

"That's a relief," Kate said over a cacophony of women's voices in the background.

I kept walking through the lobby. "How's everything going over there?"

"Everything was fine until Nadine started rearranging her bouquet and made Mack cry. He and Buster went to repair the damage she did, and I ordered more champagne."

"Good work, Kate. I'll be back in a few minutes." I started up the staircase to the executive offices. "Richard and I are going to say hi to Georgia really fast."

"Okay, but if you see Darcy, don't mention the news about Jean."

"Why not?" I stopped on the landing and waited for Richard to catch up.

"You're not going to believe this, but I just overheard the catering assistants here gossiping about a big secret Darcy's been keeping from everyone at the Fairmont," Kate said. "She and Jean were dating."

Chapter 34

"Darcy and Jean?" I almost stumbled up a step. "Are you sure?"

Richard caught me by the elbow. "What about them?"

"That's what the girls over here said," Kate assured me over the phone. "It seems like Darcy went to a lot of trouble to make sure no one at the Fairmont found out."

"I'm sure," I said. "The management isn't fond of employees dating. That's a recipe for early unemployment."

"Who's dating?" Richard hissed, jogging up the steps to keep up with me.

"Hold on," I whispered and pointed to the phone. "It's Kate."

"Exactly," Kate said. "I don't blame her for keeping it quiet, especially knowing what Mr. Elliot can be like. Too bad for Darcy her boyfriend turned out to be a dud."

I laughed. "I'd say that being a serial killer makes you a bit more than a dud in the boyfriend rating system."

"Kate's dating a serial killer?" Richard clasped his hand over his mouth.

"Hey, with some of the guys I've gone out with lately, that'd be an improvement," Kate said.

I shook my head at Richard. "No, Darcy."

"Don't mention anything to Darcy," Kate reminded me. "It might be a touchy subject."

"Got it. I'll see you in a few." I dropped the phone back in my jacket as we reached the top of the stairs.

"Kate's dating Darcy or Darcy's dating a serial killer?" Richard's voice went up a few octaves.

I grabbed Richard by the shoulders. "Keep it down. We don't want the whole lobby to know." I glanced at the bustling hotel beneath us. "Darcy's dating Jean, and Jean just got hauled away for the three murders."

"Oh." Richard pulled himself away from me. "Why didn't you say that in the first place?"

"Sorry." I offered a slightly sarcastic apology. "But don't say anything about Jean if we see Darcy. I don't want to cause a scene."

Richard made signs of locking his mouth and throwing away the key. "You know me. Discretion is my middle name."

"How could I forget?" I pushed open the glass door to the catering and sales offices. The secretary who sat at the front desk was gone, so I peeked around the doorway to the back offices.

Richard crept close behind me. "Do you know where Georgia's office is or are we going to wander aimlessly?"

"It's right down here on the left. She has a window over the alley."

"Pretty."

We walked through the maze of gray fabric cubicles that took up the majority of the floor space. It was eerily quiet since most of the sales staff had left for the weekend and only catering staff with events remained. I heard a soft humming as we reached Georgia's office door.

"Annabelle." Darcy poked her head over the cubicle divider across from Georgia's office. "What are you doing here?"

Richard shrieked and almost leapt into my arms, then glared at Darcy. "Don't jump out at people like that. You almost gave me a heart attack."

"We stopped by to welcome Georgia back to work," I explained, prying Richard off me.

Darcy came around the divider. "I'm not sure if she wants to be disturbed. . . ."

"They aren't disturbing me." Georgia threw open the door to her office. Her emerald green wrap top draped open, showing the edge of her black lace bra; her hot pink lipstick was smeared; and her hair looked like it had been through a wind tunnel. Reg sat in the chair behind her, wearing equal amounts of pink lipstick and a stunned expression.

"Good Lord." Richard averted his eyes.

"Isn't it wonderful, Annabelle?" Georgia pulled me into her office, tugging her blouse closed an inch. "It took being arrested for me to realize that what I've really been looking for has been right under my nose all this time."

"That's wonderful." I took a step back into the hall. "But we don't want to interrupt anything."

"Nonsense." Georgia threw an arm around my

shoulders, causing her shirt to fall open even more. "I have you to thank for everything. Reg told me how you questioned everyone and almost got in trouble with our GM."

"I'm glad everything turned out okay." I looked at Reg, and then nudged her. "Or should I say better than okay?"

"Can you believe he's had feelings for me for all these years and I never knew it?" Georgia whispered to me, and then blew a kiss to Reg.

"We're all happy you're out," I said. "Richard helped us with the investigation, too, you know."

Richard tried to look at Georgia without dropping his eyes to her cleavage. "Hotel catering would have been dreadfully dull without you, darling."

"I'm lucky to have such great friends." Georgia's eyes filled with tears. "And a great assistant, too. Darcy kept the place running while I was away. My office was spotless, and she even caught up with my proposals."

Darcy blushed and shook her head. "I'm relieved you're back. I don't think I could have done your job for one more day, and especially not today's wedding."

Reg stood up and looked at his watch. "That reminds me, I have to start the setup in the Colonnade."

Georgia stuck her lower lip out in a pout, and then turned to us. "Let me walk him to the door, then I'll come back and we can catch up. Make yourself comfortable in my office."

Richard swished past Reg and lowered himself into a chair. "Take your time, honey."

"I'm going to get back to work," Darcy said, stepping back toward her cubicle. "We have a few last minute changes to tonight's wedding timing."

I joined Richard in Georgia's office and walked around her desk to look out the window. It was open all the way and a breeze fluttered in, although the smell from the alley Dumpster below wasn't exactly refreshing. I pressed my nose against the screen so I could look straight down. Employee parking, loading dock, Dumpsters. Not the greatest view, but it beat a cubicle.

"Not a bad office. I like the color." Richard waved a hand at the soft green paint that covered the walls. He craned his neck to look at the shelves behind him that held wedding books, leftover unity candles, cake knives, and stacks of yarmulkes. "She's stocked up, huh?"

I sat down in Georgia's swivel chair. "Next time I'll know where to come when a client forgets the unity candle."

"Speaking of ceremonies, don't you have one to get to?"

"I still have time. They should still be doing pictures right now." I spun around in the chair. "Anyway, Kate can handle it for a few more minutes."

Richard held up a hand for me to be quiet. "Is someone humming the theme song from 'Bewitched'?"

I listened for a moment and realized that the sound came from Darcy's cubicle. I stood up and looked at the perfectly painted walls of Georgia's office. I felt like smacking myself in the head, but instead I reached for a pink paperweight on the desk and hurled it against the wall. It hit the surface with a loud thud, and pieces of plaster and pale green paint fell to the floor with it.

Richard leapt out of his chair. "Look what you've done to Georgia's wall. What on earth has gotten into you?"

"Maybe Darcy can explain," I said, motioning to the catering assistant who stood in the doorway, staring at the hole in the wall.

Chapter 35

I walked around the desk and advanced on Darcy. "Maybe you forgot the little story you told me about Georgia's fight with Henri the day he was murdered?"

Darcy remained silent, chewing on her lower lip.

"You claimed that Georgia got so enraged at Henri that she threw a paperweight at him and missed, hitting the wall in her office. One problem, though. No holes in the wall." I took a breath and continued. "Very clever way to cast doubt on Georgia's innocence."

"What's going on?" Richard snapped. "I thought we were finished with all this murder nonsense. Might I remind you, Annabelle, that you just had Jean hauled off to the police station?"

Darcy's eyes flitted to mine and burned with anger before going blank again.

"I thought we'd wrapped everything up, too," I said. "But I thought about something Jean said to me. 'Don't believe everything you see.'"

"How delightful," Richard drawled. "A pastry chef with a penchant for murder and riddles."

"I think he was talking about you." I took a step toward Darcy. "Isn't that right?"

"Her?" Richard shook his head. "But you have evidence that the three chefs killed Henri, don't you?"

"Technically, yes," I admitted. "But I have a feeling that there's more to Darcy and to these murders than meets the eye."

"So I exaggerated the story about Georgia and Henri's fight." Darcy shrugged. "So what?"

"Not only did you not want Georgia to get out of jail, you're the one who fed information and fake evidence to the cops to make her look more suspicious." I leveled a finger at her. "Who better to plant her trademark scarf for the cops to find after your boyfriend put blood on it?"

Darcy raised an eyebrow. "I knew Jean couldn't keep our relationship to himself. Men are so indiscreet."

"Tell me about it, sister." Richard sunk back down in his seat.

"Just because I'm dating Jean doesn't mean I had

anything to do with the murders," Darcy said.

"I think men have been your downfall, Darcy." I perched on the corner of the desk. "You've been covering up for your boyfriend and your father all this time."

I watched as Darcy's hands curled into fists, but her expression remained unchanged.

"Her father?" Richard asked.

"That's right," I said. "Didn't you know that Darcy is the daughter that Marcello lost years ago?"

Richard spun around in his chair. "What? Have you lost your mind, Annabelle, or are you determined to ruin me?"

"When I heard Darcy humming the theme song from 'Bewitched,' everything fell into place. How many people do you know who hum old TV theme songs?" I asked.

Richard eyed Darcy. "Well, it would explain why a girl with an Irish name looks so Italian and has questionable choice in music."

"My mother is Irish," Darcy said quietly, her voice steady. "I took her last name."

"I told you." Richard gave me a smug grin. "I knew something wasn't right from the beginning. Black Irish, my foot."

I locked eyes with Darcy and put on my best poker face. "Jean confessed to everything. How he, Emilio, and Gunter killed Henri and you set up Georgia to take the fall for them."

"Jean told you?" Darcy narrowed her eyes at me.

I nodded. "He said he wasn't going down alone."

"I knew I shouldn't have trusted him," Darcy muttered. "Men are weak."

"You father wasn't weak, though," I said. "He was behind this whole murder, wasn't he?"

Darcy burst into derisive laughter. "My father wishes he masterminded Henri's murder. No, he watched from the sidelines, as usual."

"Thank heavens." Richard brushed a hand across his forehead. "It's so hard to replace good chefs nowadays."

"But that doesn't make sense," I said. "Marcello had more motive than anyone. Henri destroyed his life."

"No, Henri destroyed my life." Darcy wrung her hands together. "Do you know what it's like to be eight years old and have your family fall apart? After he was fired, my father became obsessed with getting revenge on Henri. It was all he thought about, talked about. He couldn't find work and he became more and more bitter. Finally, my mother thought we'd be better off without him. I didn't see him for twenty years."

"So you're telling me that after all that time, Marcello didn't have anything to do with killing Henri?" I asked.

Darcy jabbed at her chest. "He may have forgotten about revenge, but I didn't."

Darcy no longer looked like the uptight, frazzled assistant I'd known. She looked calm, controlled, and a little crazy.

I edged around behind the desk. Why hadn't I seen

it before? "So you were behind all of this. You came to the Fairmont with the express purpose of killing Henri, and you waited three years to get the revenge your father never could."

"Never send a man to do a woman's job," Darcy said.

Richard started to open his mouth in protest, but took one look at Darcy and abandoned the idea. He slid out of his chair and took a step toward the door. Darcy blocked him.

"You don't understand," she said patiently. "I didn't kill Henri. I was nowhere near the murder scene."

"You convinced Jean, Gunter, and Emilio to kill him for you, though," I argued. "Jean is telling that to the police right this second."

She shut the office door and leaned against it. "Actually, I only had to convince Jean. He got the others on board. They never knew I had anything to do with it."

"Well, if you didn't actually kill anyone, I'd say there's no harm done." Richard gave a nervous laugh. "Don't you agree, Annabelle?"

I ignored him. "You may not have killed Henri, but you conspired to murder him. Was it your idea to get rid of Gunter and Emilio, too?"

"So unfortunate." Darcy frowned and pointed a finger at me. "But they couldn't be trusted not to talk, what with you snooping around and asking so many questions."

"Nice going," Richard mumbled under his breath, as

he joined me behind the desk.

"I gave you lots of warnings, Annabelle," Darcy reminded me. "You don't take hints very well, do you?"

"Don't think I haven't said exactly the same thing," Richard said.

I glared at him. "Whose side are you on, anyway?"

He avoided my eyes. "What? She makes a good point."

I turned my attention back to Darcy. "Does your father appreciate that you did his dirty work for him and you're going to go to jail for conspiracy to murder?"

"He has to be proud of me after what I did for him." Darcy's eyes darted wildly around the room. "He has to love me after the sacrifices I made for him. Sacrifices he was never willing to make for me."

Richard gave a low whistle. "Have you ever considered family therapy?"

Darcy's eyes blazed, and she slid a cake knife off the shelf next to her. "You have no idea what you're talking about, and I have no intention of going to jail."

"She's got a knife." Richard's voice came out as little more than a squeak.

Darcy advanced toward us and I backed up, treading firmly on Richard's toes.

"You can't prove that I had anything to do with the murders." Darcy leaned over the desk and swiped the knife at us. "I'm innocent."

Richard shrieked as the blade missed his face by

only inches. "May I point out that this is not the behavior of an innocent person?"

Richard and I leaned back to avoid getting cut by the flailing blade and stumbled against the window screen. It bowed with our weight, and we both lurched back into the room. Darcy started around the side of the desk, and I gave Richard a push.

"Move it!" I screamed.

Darcy lunged for us as we ran for the door, and the knife nicked Richard in the arm. He took one look at the drops of blood spreading on the sleeve of his white shirt and collapsed in a dead faint. I stumbled over him, landing on my hands and knees.

"You're not going to get away with this," I gasped as Darcy rounded the desk.

"I keep telling you." She raised the knife over her head. "I'm innocent."

"You're crazy." I scurried around the desk as she dove for me, and got behind the swivel chair. Darcy came around the corner, cursing and panting, her hair hanging in her face. Now she did look crazy. She saw me behind the chair and rushed forward, arms outstretched.

I kicked the chair away from me and it spun toward her, knocking her off balance and sending her sprawling against the window screen. The knife blade pierced the screen, and she flailed for a second before her weight ripped the screen open and she plummeted to the ground below. I cringed when her screams came to an abrupt stop.

I sat frozen in shock for a few minutes, trying to digest what had happened. I could hear screams and loud voices below me, but I couldn't force myself to move. Darcy had wasted her entire life so she could get revenge for her father and win his love? Dr. Phil would have a field day with this.

I finally tried to stand but my legs felt too weak, so I crawled shakily away from the window until I reached Richard. I rolled him over and slapped his cheeks.

His eyes fluttered open and he sat up. "What happened?"

"The short version?" I slumped against the desk. "Darcy fell out the window. She's gone."

The door swung open and Georgia gaped at us. "What on earth is going on here?" She looked around the room. "You trashed my office."

Reese appeared behind her and called over his shoulder, "The body fell from in here, guys."

"Body?" Georgia jumped when she saw Reese. "What's going on?"

"It's a long story." I took Reese's hand and let him pull me up. "Give me a second and I'll explain everything."

"What happened to your arm?" Georgia asked Richard, pointing to the blood on his shirt.

Reese turned to one of the officers who'd joined him. "Get another ambulance here. Looks like we've got a stab wound."

"Stab wound?" Richard looked down at his arm,

then his eyes rolled back in his head and he sagged to the floor again.

Georgia stuck her head out into the hall. "Where's Darcy? She was here a minute ago."

I looked from Reese to the ripped window screen and back again. "I'm afraid she stepped out."

Chapter 36

"Where have you been, Annabelle?" Kate rushed me as Richard and I stepped out of the Park Hyatt's elevator onto the ballroom level. Groomsmen in black tuxedos clustered by the door of the ballroom, handing out programs, and the familiar sounds of a string quartet came from inside. "It's ten minutes until they walk down the aisle, and we're missing a mother of the groom."

"I got here as fast as I could," I said as I appraised the setup. A towering glass vase of green viburnum dominated a round table in the foyer and made me do a double take. The Mighty Morphin Flower Arrangers had blown me away again. "Richard had to get stitches and wouldn't let me leave him."

"An exaggeration," Richard spluttered. "But I would think that my life would be a little more important than yet another wedding."

"Stitches?" Kate looked at Richard's shirt and her mouth dropped open.

Richard lowered his voice and made sure no guests

were within earshot. "I was stabbed."

"By Jean?" Kate asked.

"No, by Darcy." Richard was relishing every moment of this. "Turns out she was the brains behind the whole operation. It also turns out that she's Marcello's daughter."

"Wow." Kate looked dazed. "I missed a lot."

"Once we find the missing mother, I'll fill you in," I assured her, taking the wedding timeline out of her hands and looking at my watch.

"She was here for pictures, and then she went to her room to freshen up her makeup," Kate said. "Although between you and me if she puts on much more she's going to topple over from the weight of her eye shadow."

"Is that her?" Richard's eyes were wide as he stared behind me.

I turned around and was almost blinded by the copper crushed lamé dress advancing on me. I hadn't thought it possible to match a dress to a skin tone as perfectly as she had. She was an unnatural shade of burnished orange from her shellacked hair to her talonlike fingernails. The only spots on her body that weren't orange were her turquoise eyelids.

"What's the mother of the bride wearing?" I whispered to Kate.

"Lavender suit. No beads."

"Have they seen each other?" I hesitated to ask.

Kate nodded. "It wasn't pretty."

"This is better than reality TV," Richard said.

"Well, girls." The groom's mother tapped her watch. "Looks like it's showtime. Come on, Harold." Her husband shuffled behind her toward the ballroom.

"What happened to the grandfather?" I'd expected to see the geriatric Don Juan permanently attached to Kate.

"I had him seated early." Kate smiled mischievously. "To give him more time to get down the aisle."

I patted her on the shoulder. "Good thinking."

"Do you want to get the bridesmaids lined up while I deal with the moms and cue the—" I stopped in mid-sentence as I saw Leatrice, Ian, and Reese get off the elevator. "What are you doing here? All of you?"

Reese rolled his eyes. "I found these two snooping around the Fairmont."

Leatrice nodded eagerly. "Ian and I heard about the latest accident at the Fairmont on my police scanner and he wanted to come down and see what happened."

"We can't have them messing up our crime scene, but I recognized your neighbor right away." The side of Reese's mouth quivered until he could no longer suppress a grin. "When I mentioned that you were over here, they insisted on coming to see you."

"How thoughtful of you." I hoped he didn't miss my sarcasm.

Ian stepped in close to me and took my hand into both of his. "We heard what happened. Are you all right?"

My mouth went dry as I tried to speak. I didn't know which man made me more nervous, but I definitely

265

couldn't handle them together.

Richard sighed. "Oh for heaven's sake, she's fine. I'm the one who nearly died."

"Did you now?" Leatrice bounced over to Richard, the penguins on her sweater jiggling. "Is that blood?"

Reese cleared his throat to get my attention. "I also thought I'd tell you that I got a call from the station. Jean finally confessed to the murders and to Darcy's part in them. Apparently she was the one who managed to lift the video tape when she was giving a statement at the station."

"So she was the one giving you evidence against Georgia that day? She must have overheard us talking about the video of the murder." I tried to keep my voice steady and sound professional. "I'm glad everything turned out okay."

Reese looked at my hands clasped in Ian's, and then met my eyes for a brief moment. "I have to get back to the crime scene. Try to stay out of trouble from now on, okay, Annabelle?"

I took a tiny step back from Ian, whose gaze was now focused on Reese. I didn't want Reese to think that Ian and I were a couple when we hadn't even gone out yet, but I didn't want Ian to think that I had a thing for the detective, either. I didn't know what I wanted, but I definitely needed an aspirin from my emergency kit.

"The detective knows you pretty well, eh?" Ian said, loosening his grip on my hands.

I could feel my face getting warm. "We've worked

together before, that's all."

"Some people have a hard time staying out of trouble," Richard said under his breath, looking pointedly at me as Reese got back on the elevator. "Especially when they juggle too much at one time."

I gave Richard a kick in the shins and felt better when he yelped in pain.

"What time is it?" Kate pulled my hands away from Ian to look at my watch. "We only have three minutes."

I flipped a page in the timeline to bring me to the ceremony page. "Sorry to rush off, guys, but we have to get a bride down the aisle."

"Well, that's another thing." Kate avoided my eyes. "The bride is . . . um, here, see for yourself."

She pulled me by the elbow down the hall to the junior ballroom, with Richard, Leatrice, and Ian trailing behind. The small ballroom had been sectioned off and set up as a holding room for the bridal party. Fern sat in the midst of the celadon-clad bridesmaids dispensing dubious sex advice. The bride wore a dazed smile on her face and looked like she was on the verge of slipping off her chair.

"Is she drunk?" I hissed at Kate.

"I'd say she's snockered," Ian said.

Fern jumped up from his chair and ran over to me. "Annabelle! Don't they all look gorgeous? I mean for a bunch of tramps, of course." He burst into laughter, and all the girls joined him.

I had to live vicariously through Fern's insults. Just

once I'd like to be able to call a bridesmaid a tramp and live to tell the tale.

I noticed Fern's glassy eyes. "How much champagne did you all have?"

"Oh, it wasn't the champagne that relaxed everyone." Fern cupped his hand and leaned close to my ear. "It was the Valium I crushed up in it that really took the edge off Nadine."

"I've always wanted to try Valium." Leatrice eyed the empty glasses. "I hear it's coming back into fashion."

Sometimes I really wondered where Leatrice got her information.

"You drugged the bride?" I rubbed my temples. Darcy had been a piece of cake compared to this.

"How much did you have?" Richard asked Fern as he watched him lean against the wall with one arm.

"Only a teensy slip or two." Fern slid down the wall to the floor.

I stepped over Fern and walked over to Nadine, shaking her by the shoulders. "It's time to get married."

Nadine raised her head and gave me a huge vacant smile. "Congratulations."

I pulled her up by her arms and propped her against me. "No, Nadine. You're getting married, remember?"

"If you think I should," she slurred.

At least they weren't reciting their own vows, I reminded myself.

"Bridesmaids line up in the order we rehearsed,"

Kate called from the door in her best drill sergeant voice. "Don't forget your bouquets."

The girls shuffled into line and followed Kate out the door. I grabbed Nadine's bouquet off the table and handed it to Richard as I tried to walk her into the lobby.

Richard stared at the green pod bouquet. "What on earth . . . ?"

I held up a hand. "Don't ask."

"This is so exciting." Leatrice clapped her hands. "What can I do?"

"Grab her train so it doesn't get all twisted," I instructed, motioning to the back of Nadine's cathedral-length dress.

"Let me give you a hand with her." Ian winked at me as he took the other side of the sagging bride. "This isn't how I imagined spending time with you, but it's not so bad."

"I'm really sorry that I was out when you came by last night." I tried to keep my voice low so Richard wouldn't overhear. "Kate and I got stuck at work."

Ian gave me a playfully suspicious look. "So you weren't out with another fellow?"

I shook my head and felt my cheeks start to warm.

"I told him that I'd be shocked if you were on a date," Leatrice chimed in.

"Thanks." I turned to shoot daggers at Leatrice, who happily hummed "The Wedding March" as we lurched down the hall. I said a prayer of thanks that the mother of the bride had already been seated and couldn't see the motley crew dragging her daughter down the hall.

When we reached the doorway to the ballroom, Kate was sending the maid of honor down the aisle. She closed the ballroom doors, and I passed the bride off to her startled father, pulling the blusher over her face. Kate and I each held one of the door handles and waited for the music to change while Richard placed the bouquet in the bride's hand.

"Go slow," I whispered to Nadine's father as the trumpet began the processional fanfare and Leatrice unfurled the train behind them.

Kate and I threw open the double doors simultaneously and watched the bride and her father shuffle diagonally down the aisle before we closed the ballroom doors behind them. I slumped against the door.

Ian leaned next to me. "Boy, your weddings sure are something special. Dead bodies, drunk brides—"

I elbowed him lightly. "Hey, all our weddings aren't like this."

"Sometimes there are drunks *and* dead bodies," Richard said, smirking at me.

"I wouldn't mind being a wedding planner." Leatrice stood on her tiptoes to look through the peephole in the ballroom door. "And I'll bet it's even easier when the bride is awake."

"Not always." Between confronting a murderer and getting a doped-up bride down the aisle, I felt like crawling in bed for a week.

"That wasn't so bad," Kate said. "Why didn't we

think of sedating our brides before, huh?"

Richard stared at Kate. "Because it's illegal?"

"You know what they say." Kate grinned. "All's bare in love and war."

Center Point Publishing
600 Brooks Road ● PO Box 1
Thorndike ME 04986-0001 USA

(207) 568-3717

**US & Canada:
1 800 929-9108**